Multiple Shades of Gray

CRAIG SPENCE FINDS A KILLER HIDING AMONG RETIREES

Multiple Shades of Gray

Gray

CRAIG SPENCE FINDS A KILLER HIDING AMONG RETIREES

JR CONWAY

Copyright © 2023 by JR Conway

All rights reserved. No part of this publication may be reproduced, distributed, or transmitted in any form or by any means, including photocopying, recording, or other electronic or mechanical methods, without the prior written permission of the copyright owner and the publisher, except in the case of brief quotations embodied in critical reviews and certain other noncommercial uses permitted by copyright law. For permission requests, write to the publisher, addressed "Attention: Permissions Coordinator," at the address below.

CITIOFBOOKS, INC.
3736 Eubank NE Suite A1
Albuquerque, NM 87111-3579
www.citiofbooks.com

Hotline: 1 (877) 389-2759
Fax: 1 (505) 930-7244

Ordering Information:
Quantity sales. Special discounts are available on quantity purchases by corporations, associations, and others. For details, contact the publisher at the address above.

Printed in the United States of America.

ISBN-13:   Softcover   978-1-960952-04-2
                eBook   978-1-960952-05-9

Library of Congress Control Number: 2023907136

Contents

I

For Craig retirement took some getting used to but not for Martha, she enjoyed it immensely. She no longer spent her days wondering what Craig was getting involved in, and the nights when he was out, with her heart in her throat waiting for him to come home or call her, so she knew he was all right.

She had always wanted to travel and now spent lots of time researching places to go and planning trips that the two would enjoy together. One trip that they both really enjoyed was a cruise from Seattle Washington to Alaska. They sailed deep into the Gulf of Alaska and Prince William Sound. They spent seven days traveling from Anchorage to Vancouver, B.C. stopping in historic port cities like Ketchikan, Juneau, and Skagway. The scenery was breathtakingly beautiful.

On this trip, Craig spent a lot of time at the ship's rails and on the balcony of their cabin. There seemed to always be a group of colorful dolphins racing alongside the ship, and in the evenings there were all sorts of colorful reflections from the ship's lights dancing in the aqua water. Several afternoons while they were lounging on the deck, a member of the crew had alerted passengers that a pod of whales had been sighted and that they would be coming up on the port or starboard side. On one occasion the whales were just leisurely cruising on the surface, blowing spray into the air at different intervals. At another time, it was as though they were putting on a show, breaching and rolling as the passengers lined the rails and wondered at the performance.

Another thing that they found fascinating was what appeared to be the preferred or necessary mode of Travel in Alaska. Seaplanes were everywhere. The skies around the port cities were always abuzz with the sounds of planes. Watching them take off and the land was a great pastime when the ship was docked at a port city.

Between trips, Martha and Craig made it a point to get to know their neighbors at the Green River Senior Manor and they came to enjoy visiting and learning the life stories of other people, which were so much different than their own. Getting to know people generally occurred at mealtime. Craig enjoyed watching the servers flit around the tables taking people's orders and delivering meals. It was like watching an orchestrated musical.

At lunch on one occasion, Craig and Martha sat at a table with an Asian lady. Martha started the conversation.

"Hello, my name is Martha, and this is my husband Craig, and your name is---?"

"My Name is Tei; Tei Chi, people call me Tess, it is so nice of you to sit with me," was the reply.

Tess was slender in appearance, dressed in a white turtle neck sweater and black pants. The sweater really accented her salt and pepper hair that was cropped and styled from her chin around her head to her chin on the opposite side. She had very dark eyes that set far apart from a small straight nose that sat above a perfectly formed small mouth.

"How long have you been here," Craig asked.

" I think maybe a couple of weeks," Tess responded.

"Craig and I were among the first to move here," Martha related. "I've always wanted to travel so we've been gone a lot. Where are you from Tess?"

"I was born in a small village in Hainan province in China," Tess began. "When I was around five years of age my family moved to the US. I was raised in San Francisco. Have you always lived in Wyoming?"

"Born and raised," Martha replied. "I worked for the county until I married Craig, and he was the county sheriff for many years. What did you do and how did you end up here?"

"I studied political science at Stanford University and eventually was awarded a position at the embassy of China in San Francisco. A part of my family ancestry is here. Many years passed in my family history and members were brought here to work in the mines. There are descendants here and I came to Wyoming after I retired to connect. The owners of the Golden Dragon Restaurant in Rock Springs are a family of long distance. I worked in the restaurant until I had a stroke, and now I live here."

Then there was Norman, a large man with an extended belly. Norman was disfigured on the left side of his face; his left eye was partially closed, and his neck and his hands showed evidence that he had been severely burned. Craig noticed that Norman had a scar on the brow above his right eye. Only an ex-boxer would notice that. It was at an evening meal that the meeting had occurred and again it was Martha who initiated the conversation and managed the introductions.

"Hello sir, may we sit with you? My name is Martha, and this is my husband Craig."

"There's plenty of room, sit down," was the response. Craig noticed that he spoke out the side of his mouth because of the scarring.

"Don't recall seeing you around since we've been here," Craig said. "I see you have a name tag that they gave you, it says Norman, Norman Clayborn. "Nice to meet you Norman."

"Don't come down often," Norman said.

"You a Wyomingite?" Craig asked.

"No. Came from back east," said Norman.

"What brought you out here?" Martha asked.

"You people sure ask a lot of questions don't cha?" Norman seemed annoyed.

"Just trying to be neighborly and get to know you," Craig said. "If you'd rather not talk we can handle that." The rest of the meal was eaten in silence. When Norman was through and got up to leave he put his hand on Craig's shoulder and spoke.

"Don't mean to be rude fella. Just don't like it when people start asking a lot of questions." When he was gone Martha said. "Now that's a real piece of work. Course we don't know what he went through to get all scarred up like that."

" Some people just don't like people prying into their lives," Craig surmised as he wiped his mouth with a napkin. "I suppose we won't run into too many of those."

After one of their trips, they noticed Mertel, the conservationist who was part of a couple they had first met at the Manor, sitting alone. Early on they had spent a lot of time getting to know her and Paul, her husband.

Mertel had grown up in Pennsylvania and was a high school sophomore when her dad got a job as the director of the Casper Chamber of Commerce. After high school, she went to the University of Wyoming in Laramie where she got a Bachelor of Science degree in Conservation Science. She met Paul at a conference in Green River pertaining to conservation matters concerning the Flaming Gorge Reservoir. He was the City Attorney for Green River at the time. She fell in love with him and the town and vowed to live there if she ever got the chance. When he got a job in Kalispel Montana she went with him.

Paul grew up in Ogden, Utah, and served twenty years in the Air Force as a JAG Officer (Judge Advocate General). Practicing law in the military made it easy to qualify for lawyer jobs when he got out. The last job of his career was in Kalispell, Montana as a Public Defender. He enjoyed that job because he never knew what the case was going to be. Mertel got a job as a conservation officer during that time. They both retired at the same time and were able to fulfill Mertel's dream and move to Green River, Wyoming. When Martha saw Mertel sitting alone she lead the way to sit with her.

"Hi Mertel, Where's Paul?" Martha said in greeting. She then noticed that Mertel's eyes were puffy, and they began to fill when she saw Martha. Mertel got out of her seat and hugged Martha as she began to sob.

"What has happened," Martha asked. Mertel controlled herself and sat and wiped her eyes with a napkin before speaking.

"Paul passed away while you were gone," she began. "I didn't know where you and Craig were staying, and I didn't know how to contact you. The night that we dropped you off at the airport, we decided to stop at the Dairy Queen in town on our way back. We were just sitting in the car enjoying our cones when he suddenly said to me, "I don't feel good." She paused a minute to let her emotions settle down before continuing. "I noticed he was pale, like a pasty condition. I told him to let me drive and that we were going to the hospital.

When we got there I ran in and got help to get him in and they had to physically take him out of the car. He was unconscious. They took him straight to surgery. He had had a massive heart attack. He died on the table," she softly began to sob again. "I couldn't help him," she said. Martha took Mertel in her arms and just held her, no one spoke for a long time, and it was Craig who broke the silence.

"Damned!" He exclaimed. He got up from the table and walked through the lobby and out the front doors.

Craig bought himself a Minolta camera with lenses. He had often seen herds of wild horses, antelope, elk, and deer as he traveled around the county. He had decided to spend time taking pictures. To support this new hobby he found a Willis jeep that was just what he needed to go cross country.

Martha renewed her relationship with the daughters of Steve Lolly, Marla, and Milly. The girls, now out of school and building lives for themselves, came to visit often and they went on shopping sprees together. Sometimes they just hung out. Martha was like an adopted grandmother.

Marla had decided that she wanted to pursue a law degree. The University of Wyoming offered degrees in several areas of jurisprudence. To afford to go, she decided to work for a couple of years and take some pre-law courses at night at the community college in Rock Springs. To facilitate her pursuit she managed to get a job with a Commuter Airline as a ticket agent.

Milly Survived the trauma of her encounter with Jess Preston, the drug dealer that had taken advantage of her in a sexual way at the school. For months she had feared that she might be pregnant and was so depressed that she nearly flunked out of school. Because of the absence of any evidence that penetration had occurred, the county attorney pursued charges of sexual assault and sexual abuse of a minor. Through a plea bargain, Jess had pleaded guilty, and everyone involved was relieved that there was no trial.

Milly had no desire to seek higher education and had gotten a job with the Wyoming Conservation Corps. She enjoyed being out of doors, planting trees, counting migratory birds, mending fences, and repairing hiking trails in the national forests all of which she felt was neat stuff.

Martha took advantage of the policies of the Green River Senior Manor, which allowed residents to invite guests to meals, and had the girls and their dad over for dinner one evening. The girls were jabbering away about their jobs and Steve, their dad was the bearer of sad news. Harry, the deputy who became Sheriff after Craig, had been diagnosed with stage four prostate cancer and it had moved to other organs.

"I've pretty much been seeing things through for him at the department," Steve related. He's planning to resign in the coming week. Now that the girls are grown and doing their own thing, I'm ready. I can do that job, so I plan to ask to be appointed interim sheriff until they hold a special election."

"Marla, what thinks thou of your job with the airline? Martha was asking. "Is it something you would recommend to a friend maybe?"

"If someone wanted something in the interim, yes," Marla replied. "you see, there are only two flights during weekdays, and one on Saturday and Sunday, so I have a lot of free time, but the pay is not career inspiring."

"And you Milly?" How do you feel about what you do," Martha asked.

"I couldn't be happier," Milly replied enthusiastically. "The Conservation Corps is a Non-Profit and gets all of its funding through grants and donations, so the pay is basically minimum wage. For me, doing what I do couldn't be more rewarding. I'm able to help with expenses at home and maintain a low-key social life, I'm happy."

"You've got to be one proud papa, Steve," Craig said. "The God of families has been good to ya."

"Sometimes I have to pinch myself, Boss," remarked Steve. "There were some really tough times, and together we pulled through. A lot of the credit for where we are goes to you and Martha, you hired me on when I had no experience and Martha cared for Marla and Milly when I couldn't afford help. There's no way we'll ever be able to thank you folks enough." Marla put her arms around Martha and snuggled up cheek to cheek while Milly reached over and tugged on Craig's ear three times.

Martha had arranged a trip to travel across the country on a train. This was a trip that Craig had suggested. They were going to take the California Zephyr from Denver Colorado through such scenic towns as Fraser, Granby, and Glenwood Springs, Colorado, and would be treated to such scenic areas as the Sierra Nevada's Donner Pass, Wasatch Range east of Salt Lake City, areas that neither of them had ever seen.

On the morning they were to leave for Denver, they had breakfast with Rose Carlson, a woman of some girth, and who suffered from a spinal condition that caused her to bend forward, almost ninety degrees when standing or walking. Her white hair was very thin and bounced and floated when she walked. She just allowed it to hang straight down around her head to her shoulders. Rose had a very outgoing personality and was always eager to engage people in conversation. Martha and Craig were already seated at a table when Rose approached.

"May I join you, folks?" She asked, looking up with a broad smile and an inquisitive expression on her face.

"Of course," Marth spoke up. "We'd love to have you dine with us." Rose slid the cane she used under the table and with some difficulty managed to seat herself in an empty chair.

"My name is Rose, Rose Carlson," she introduced herself. "I've seen you around every now and then but have never had the opportunity to meet you until now. I've only been here a few months. I moved here from California to be near my son who has a job with a mining company here. Where did you come from?"

"I'm afraid we didn't come from anywhere," Martha said. "We were both born and raised here in Wyoming. I'm Martha Spence and this is my husband Craig. We were one of the first residents to move in here. I'm so glad that you chose to sit with us today. It must have been a culture shock coming from California to the high desert of Wyoming."

"Not at all," Rose responded with a giggle. "I was living in a single-wide mobile home in the Needles area-have either of you been to Needles California?"

"Not I," Martha responded. "To my knowledge neither has Craig."

"No, me neither," Craig chimed in.

"Well, Needles is in the Mojave Desert," Rose explained. "It's near the borders of Arizona and Nevada. At one time, years ago – if you drove across the country to or from California you had to use Highway 40 which runs right through Needles. I suppose the population today is a little over three thousand- hot and dry, the average temperature there in the summer is one hundred seven degrees. I can't remember the last time it rained in Needles. So no, coming here was an upgrade. It's beautiful here."

"I hope I don't offend you," Craig was apologetic. "I notice that you sort of bend in the middle when you walk. Is it the result of some injury you got in an accident or a birth defect or what?"

"Not offended at all," Rose replied. "Glad you asked, Most people just stare. I have a severe case of Camptocormia or better known as Bent Spine Syndrome. It's an abnormal flexion of the trunk. When I lay down I stretch out to a respectable five foot nine inches. No, I was not born this way, it developed over time." The conversation was interrupted by a server standing by to take their orders. After each had done so Rose picked up where she had left off.

"I was the Magistrate Judge in Needles for a little over a decade and then was voted out as my condition became less accepted by the population – that's my assessment not stated fact. There are several people here who have lesser cases of Bent Spine Syndrome. Tell me about you folks. What did you do before you became people of leisure."

" I've lived in Wyoming most of my life," Craig began. "Spent a short stint in the navy a while back and was sheriff of this county until a few years ago. Martha here, put up with me all those years and was my greatest supporter."

"Wow! Rose exclaimed. "I'll bet you have a lot of interesting stories to tell."

"There were times when I was concerned about him," Martha said. "Over the years I realized eventually that he knew how to take care of himself and get the best possible result out of a situation. The fact that he was able to do the job for so long is testimony to the confidence people had in him." Their breakfasts were delivered and there was less small talk after that.

The train trip was most relaxing, and they both spent much of the trip in the observation car, taking in the scenery and the different landscapes that neither was aware of- the crew catered to their every whim, and the food, though a little expensive, was nice. They had purchased a sleeper cabin so when the train was on a siding, Martha spent the layovers in her bunk reading. On a two-hour layover in Salt Lake, where there was a crew change, Craig bought a magazine from a newsstand to help pass the time. He had selected a *True Detective*.

Across the glossy cover of the magazine in large yellow letters was the main story. ***"The unsolved case of the mystery body."*** The picture on the cover showed a burned-out building which appeared to have been a house and the pictures of a man and a woman identifying them as the married couple that lived there. The fire had occurred ten years ago.

Craig browsed through the story, the jest of which was that the law enforcement agencies had investigated a fire that had occurred in a suburb of Evanston, Indiana. They had discovered the remains of two people. Both had been severely burned in the fire and the medical examiner and forensic team used coronal plane reconstruction, CT-type imaging, and post-mortem computed tomography, a diagnostic imaging technique popular in forensic pathology, to aid in the investigation and identification of the deceased.

Investigators determined that one of the bodies was female and was identified as Mercy Tomlin, the thirty-five-year-old wife of Thomas Tomlin who had occupied the residence for seven years. There was evidence that the female had endured several stab wounds to the back, and it was determined that death had occurred prior to the fire.

The second body was that of a male and was initially assumed to probably be that of Thomas Tomblin. A partially burned wallet found at the scene contained a driver's license and credit cards belonging to Thomas Tomblin and a pick-up truck parked on the street in front of the house was registered to Thomas Tomblin. The pathologist determined that the corpse of the male also had sustained stab wounds and was deceased prior to the blaze. Dental records, however, failed to confirm that the remains were those of Thomas Tomblin. Who was he? If the remains were not those of Thomas Tomblin where was he? Craig put the magazine in the pocket of one of their travel cases intending to continue reading the story at the next layover or when they returned home.

Craig and Martha returned to the airport in Rock Springs on a beautiful Friday afternoon and were picked up by Mertel who drove them back to the Senior Manor in Green River. On the way, Craig announced his plans for the following week.

"You know," he began. "The weather looks like it's going to hold all through next week and I think I'll go find a herd of horses or some antelope and take some pictures."

"That's a great idea," Martha agreed. "It will get you out of my hair while I put things back together." Turning to Mertel she continued. "why don't you go with him? I don't think he should be out there alone and it's the sort of thing you are familiar with, and it will get you out of that apartment of yours."

"Hadn't thought of that," Craig commented. "Would you like to do that Mertel?"

"Are you sure you want a stick-in-the-mud like me tagging along?"

"Heck, it'll be good for you, and you can keep me from getting into trouble. You got any roughing stuff?"

"I still have boots and some shirts and pants from my conservation days," Mertel related.

"Good, let's plan on Tuesday of next week. We'll get out on those Plains north of White Mountain around six in the morning and see what we find."

White Mountain is a standout landmark north of Rock Springs and Green River. From the top, you could see several other mountain ranges and an area larger that the state of Massachusetts. The face of the mountain was made up of sandstone, and the rock appeared to be white as seen from Rock Springs and the town of Green River. Dirt roads and trails dissected the top of its vast expanse.

At the mid-day meal on Sunday, Craig, Martha, and Mertel were joined by a delightful lady who was probably a little over five feet tall and wore bright red lipstick which accented her engaging smile. She had a full head of white hair which was cut above the ears and sort of a duck tail at the back of her neck. As she approached Craig noticed that she wore a special type of shoe on one foot and there was a bulge around her waist. He assumed it to be a brace of some kind.

"Hey yall," she said as she approached the table. "Mind if I join you? "

"Be our guest," Craig invited. "I'm Craig, my wife Martha, and our friend Mertel."

"I'm Cora," the little lady said as she slid into the empty chair. "Cora Julie, pronounced like the month -July." She laughed as she explained, and it was a jolly laugh that turned heads. "I've seen you around Mertel, but I don't think I've seen you two before," she nodded toward Craig and Martha.

"We've been traveling a lot," Martha responded. "In fact, we just got back from a train trip across the country. Have you ever done that?"

"No, I've been taking care of my husband for the past few years and when he was active he worked for a food distribution company and was gone most of the time while I raised our kids."

"How many young ones did you raise?" Craig asked.

"Two boys," Cora said. "One is a surveyor with one of the mines and the other is a pilot for a commuter airline. I don't see him very often but the one at the mine comes by two or three times a week."

"Is he what brought you to Wyoming," Mertel asked.

"Not really, I lived in Douglas Wyoming for a number of years, but when my husband got sick my son, the one in the mines, thought it best that we move down here."

The conversation was light and jovial throughout the meal, the women chattering and learning about one another's lives before ending up at the Manor.

On Tuesday, Craig loaded his camera equipment in the back of his jeep and was off with Mertel riding shotgun right at sunrise High wispy cirrus clouds floated in the sky and the rising sun reflected its light on their edges. Above them were the pearly white contrails from the early flights of several airlines, the planes looking like silver bullets streaking across the sky.

II

Once on the mountain, Craig drove along a ridge until he had a clear view of the valley below and sure enough there was a herd of horses. He estimated there were maybe twenty adults and he counted seven colts that appeared to be about a year old. They were multi-colored. Some were brown and white, all brown, and several were palominos. There were some grays but very few blacks. Mertel spoke up.

"Look across the valley on that Little rise," she pointed out of the passenger window to their right front. A couple hundred yards or so beyond the herd Craig spotted a large buckskin, standing majestically and looking in their direction. He pulled his jeep behind a small rock formation and stopped.

"We're out of his line of sight right now," he said to Mertel. "He is on guard and nervous so let's set up the tripod just at the edge of these rocks and get a couple of pictures before he moves the herd."

The herd was moving very slowly along the valley floor, peacefully grazing along and Craig waited with his telephoto lens mounted until he could get a shot with the Stallion overlooking his charges. Mertel took a second camera, steadied it on a rock, and took some wide-angle shots incorporating the landscape surrounding the horses.

The Stallion soon had all he could take of the situation and ran down from his perch, leaving a cloud of dust in his wake. Craig was excited at the shots he was able to get as the buckskin approached the herd at a full gallop and led them through a draw on the far side of the valley and out of sight. Craig and Mertel returned the equipment to the back seat of the jeep and Craig drove slowly along the ridge in hopes of finding other herds.

Martha busied herself unpacking the luggage they'd used on the train trip. There was laundry to do and some items to be taken later to the dry cleaners. She found the magazine that Craig had saved and placed it on the nightstand on his side of the bed. She was loading clothes into the washing machine when the telephone located on the wall in the kitchen began to ring. It had rung about five times before she got to it.

"Hello," she said.

"It's Marla," Came the response. Her voice sounded strangely strained. "Martha, have you by chance seen Milly?"

"No dear, why do you ask?" Martha sat down in one of the kitchen chairs. She had a feeling that she was about to get some bad news.

"Milly didn't come home from work last night," Marla related. "The people she works with told us that she left at about six yesterday evening, heading home. Everyone had changed into street clothes, Milly in a pair of jeans, sneakers, and a blue jean shirt. They all pulled out at the same time. Milly was driving her robin egg blue colored Toyota 4Runner. We've had people looking all along the roads leading out of Seedskadee Wildlife Refuge where she was working yesterday."

"Has she not come home from work before," Martha asked.

"No, never," Marla replied. "We had made reservations for dinner last night- something bad must have happened to her."

"It is rather strange," Martha agreed. "Knowing Milly as we do, and how adventurous she is, I'd think there is an explanation. Craig is out this morning looking for stuff to take pictures of, I'll get him on the CB and let him know what has happened. I'm sure he'd want to get involved. Keep the faith dear, I'll get back to you."

Martha had never used the radio, but she had heard Craig talking to his coffee clutch buddies. The base set was on a small stand in the living room. It was on so all she had to do was key the mic and talk.

"Craig can you hear me," She said into the mic. She waited a few moments and then he responded.

"I hear you Doll, come on," was the response.

"Milly is missing. She didn't come home from work last night. Everyone is looking for her," Martha related.

"10-4," Craig responded. "I'll head back to town and see if I can be of help. Let Steve know that I'll be coming out." Martha did as Craig had asked…

While Milly was driving through the reserve counting Crain nests, she had come across a dirt road that crossed the waters of the Green River and appeared to lead to the top of White Mountain. If that road went all the way across it would save her lots of time driving home after work, she thought. Using the binoculars, she used to count the nest she could see the road go over the crest of the mountain. She decided to check it out when she got off work.

After crossing the river, the dirt road had several switchbacks as it wound its way up the incline. There were few vehicle tracks that she could see and those that did stand out appeared to be from four-wheelers. Her 4runner did just fine with the climb. When she reached the crest the road intersected with another, and a small wooden sign read White Mountain Road with arrows pointing in both directions. She turned right on White Mountain road because it was toward home.

It had been recently graded so she could clip along at thirty-five miles an hour comfortably. White Mountain Road had been laid out right along the mountain's rim and she could look to the west and see Interstate 80 far out in the valley, the town of Green River, and the river as it meandered through. As she rounded a turn in the road she looked back and could see Pilot Butt, A rock mound that extended high above the plains around it. Folklore has it that pilots who flew the mail years ago used the butte as a navigation aid.

When she turned her attention back to the road a deer stood directly in her path. Instinctively she slammed on her brakes, turned sharply to the right and the 4Runner went into a sideways skid; the left rear slamming into the animal; the rear end skidded toward the edge of the road; the right front wheel crossed the small ridge of dirt and rock left by the grader and the 4Runner began to tumble down the side of the mountain; end over end, bouncing off large rocks, leaving pieces of the vehicle in its path. It came to rest in a crevasse a considerable distance down the mountain's face…

The little used road that Craig had been cruising intersected with White Mountain road and he turned onto it. As he drove along his mind wandered over the many cases of missing people that had come to his attention over the years. Some he remembered had ended tragically while others had had pleasant endings. He had always felt that as Milly grew into adulthood that she could pretty well look out for herself, but she would never go off without letting her dad or her sister know what she was up to. His gut was telling him that something bad had happened to that little lady.

Rounding one of the many corners of the road Craig had to break hard to avoid the carcass of a deer in the road.

"Too bad," Mertel commented. "Wonder why whoever struck it didn't move it out of the road."

"Judging from those tracks, they might not have been able to, Look! They go over the side. I'm going to get out and take a look, and if I see anything I'll shimmy down the side, it's not really steep. you stay here in case we need to radio for help."

As Craig walked over to the side of the road where the tracks went through the small berm, he could see wreckage strewn down the mountainside. Then he spotted it, the mangled light blue car nose down in the crevasse, about fifty-seventy or so yards below the road.

"Get on that radio Mertel," Craig called up as he stood against a rock halfway to the wreckage. "Get ahold of somebody, anybody that answers, and have them get the rescue people up here, I can see a leg sticking out the side of the wreckage. We're about a mile and a half west of highway 191 on White Mountain Road." He then skidded and slid his way down to the wreckage.

As he leaned against the car for the support he could see that the leg of a person inside had become trapped between the door and the door frame. There was no shoe on the foot, and it had swollen to the size of a small football. When he looked inside there was a person dressed in jeans and a blue shirt lying awkwardly between the seats and the vehicle console, with the left leg wedged between the top of the steering wheel and the dash and the right leg sticking out and trapped by the driver's door.

One arm, the right, was caught between the dual seats, and the left was stuck beneath the person. Craig reached in through the driver's side window to brush back the hair and the dirt from the person's face. It was Milly. Her face was bruised, and he could see the left eye was swollen and there was a large goose egg on the side of her forehead. She was still breathing, ever so lightly. He didn't dare try to move her, but he spoke to her.

"Milly, if you can hear me, it's Craig- if you can hear me you're gonna be okay. Just keep hanging on doll, we're gonna get you out of here, just hang on," he said. There was no indication that Milly heard him, but he kept talking to her in case she did.

It seemed like forever, but a fire truck finally appeared on the road above. Men were scampering out of it and grabbing equipment. Craig yelled up to them.

"you're gonna need special equipment, her leg is caught between the door and the frame." One of the firefighters scampered back up the hill and pulled a black box out of one of the truck's compartments and took out a hydraulic rescue tool.

"Martha, We found her," Craig was saying on the radio, There was no response so he said again. "We found her Martha."

"Oh, thank heaven," Martha responded". Is she all right?"

"Rescue is with here now," Craig advised. "Tell you more later, out."

Craig and Mertel watched as the rescue team worked meticulously, one group providing lifesaving care to Milly while others worked to free her leg. After almost an hour, they had her out and Craig could see an IV bottle being held up by one of the crew, a good sign he thought, and they were applying inflatable splints to her arms and leg. Then Craig heard the sound of a helicopter in the distance. He looked up and saw that it was heading straight for the crash site. When it arrived he watched as it came to a hover; Milly was placed in a basket and hoisted into the aircraft; and it headed back toward Rock Springs.

Marla had relayed the message from Martha to her dad, Steve Lolly, and he left his office on the run, using his marked unit, lights flashing and siren blaring he had made record time traveling the eleven miles to the hospital in Rock Springs. Milly was already in the ER being evaluated when he arrived. The female person at the admitting desk recognized Steve and could see the impatience as he paced.

" Mr. Lolly," she said. "It's going to be a little while till we know anything; can I get you a water or coffee while you wait?"

"No thanks," Steve responded.

"Do you know the patient that arrived by helicopter?" She was trying to engage in conversation.

"That's my daughter in there," Steve related.

"Oh dear"! the lady exclaimed. "I'll let them know that you are here, maybe they'll have some news for you." She exited through an adjoining door to the ER.

Steve had no idea how much time had passed before a person in a white coat came through the same door the admitting person had gone through.

"Hi, I'm doctor Messenger, the ER doctor on duty today, and you are….?"

"I'm Steve Lolly, that's my daughter you have in there," Steve responded.

"Well Steve, your daughter is a very lucky young lady. She sustained some injuries but from the pictures of the accident that the firefighters showed me it could have been much worse."

"How is she?" Steve asked.

" So far we know that she suffered a concussion, a broken right collar bone, and a broken tibia in the right leg. She is dehydrated and there could be other problems in that leg due to the length of time there was restricted blood flow. She's undergoing a scan to see what else might have been damaged. An orthopedic specialist is on his way over to further evaluate the leg. That's all I have for you right now."

"If only she had worn her seat belt," Steve thought aloud.

"Sir," Dr. Messenger said, as he laid his hand on Steve's shoulder, "From the way that car was damaged, had she been strapped in that driver's seat, I'd probably be determining the time of death. Count your blessings." The doctor turned and left the way he'd come.

Martha, Marla, Steve, Craig, and Mertel all had gathered in the waiting room awaiting some word about Milly. Steve was sitting between Craig and Mertel, Martha sat with an arm around Marla who was resting her head on Martha's shoulder. Steve got up and began to pace. It was Mertel who broke the tense silence.

"It's not going to help Mr. Lolly, wearing down the tile like that. You know, I could use a cup of coffee. Why don't you come with me, and we'll go down the hall to the cafeteria and get some coffee for everybody?

"Good idea," Martha agreed. "Craig, why don't you go with them and help carry the cups? It'll only take a moment and you can walk off some of the nervous energy."

The group had only been back a few minutes when Dr. Messenger and another man in a white coat entered the waiting room. Messenger spoke to Steve.

"We met earlier Steve," he said. "But it looks like you have family here."

"Yeh," Steve began. "We have Sheriff Spence, retired, and Mertel here who came across the wreckage and found Milly; Mrs. Spence who helped me raise my daughters, Milly and her sister, Marla there."

"Nice meeting you all," Messenger began. "Well, we have some good news and some not-so-good news. Dr. Mason will explain in a minute. As I told you, Steve, we knew that she had suffered a concussion, a fractured collar bone, and a fractured tibia of the right leg. The good news is that other than some scrapes and bruises, we didn't find any other serious injuries. With time she should recover nicely. Dr. Mason here is an Orthopedic Surgeon and will talk about the leg fracture." Dr. Mason began by pulling up the left leg of his trousers.

"The tibia is the bone that runs from the knee to the ankle," he said. "Because it's so strong it generally takes a severe trauma like a fall or a car accident to break it. If it is fractured it will generally take surgery to repair the damage. There was severe tissue damage caused to the leg both by it being trapped in the wreckage and the restricted blood flow for some time. Your tibia also supports lots of important muscles, tendons, nerves, and ligaments. I'll be working with other specialists to assess the damage sustained there. Depending on what we find during exploratory surgery will dictate if when and how I'll be able to repair the fracture."

"You said if," Steve recalled. "Does that mean she could lose part or all of her leg?"

"A blocked blood vessel or restricted blood flow for some time can cause tissue to decay and die," Dr. Mason said. "This is referred to as Gangrene. There is no cure. The only treatment in such a case is to surgically remove the affected part. We'll be able to assess the situation much better after the swelling subsides and we can do exploratory surgery. In the meantime, she'll be in ICU where she can be watched and await the results of all the tests to come in."

"Unless you have other questions, we'll see you when we have more information," Dr. Messenger said. "We'll contact you Steve as soon as we know. Make sure that admittance has all of your correct contact information, Good day." And he and Dr. Mason left the room.

Martha took charge of things and made arrangements with the charge nurse at the intensive care unit for a member of the family to be with Milly. It was decided that Martha would take the mornings, Marla would be at the bedside in the afternoons and Craig would take the night shift. This freed Steve to take care of his day job. Mertel volunteered to be the gofer for anyone that had chores or unexpected tasks that needed doing.

Craig took the true detective magazine with him on his first night at Milly's bedside. The nurse was in the room when he relieved Marla. Milly was sleeping so he had to speak in a whisper.

"How's the patient," he asked the nurse.

"She's holding her own," the nurse replied. "She'll be in and out. The doctors want us to manage her pain at a level that just takes the edge off. They want her to be able to respond to questions and they don't want her sedated to the point that we can't monitor the results of the concussion. I just put some pain medication in her IV. Make yourself comfortable; I, the lab techs and the nurse aids taking blood pressure will be in and out all night. Neither she nor you will get much sleep," she said with a chuckle.

Craig pulled up a chair on Milly's left side. The right arm was tied across her chest so she couldn't move it. There were tubes and wires going in what seemed all directions. Her right leg was elevated on a pillow and a cable went from her right foot to a clamp at the foot of the bed. The bruises on her face were beginning to turn blue and dark red. Her left eye was swollen and closed. The goose egg he'd seen at the wreck was gone and only a raised bump was in its place.

He settled in with the magazine story; the extent of the investigative effort and the evidence that led to the misidentification of the male body. The only known factors were that there were two homicides, and the fire was apparently set to cover the deed. His reading was interrupted by someone pulling on his ear. Milly was awake.

"Hi doll," he said. "They tell me you're gonna make it."

"I heard you," her lips hardly moved when she spoke, and her voice was raspy.

"what? When do you mean?" Craig asked, somewhat puzzled.

"I heard you talking to me," Milly said. "Thank you. I hurt all over. My leg---," and she closed her eyes and seemed to be slipping back into a troubled sleep.

As Craig returned his attention to his magazine he noticed that the way he held it in his hand, his thumb was covering half of Thomas Tomblin's face. He took his thumb off the picture several times to be sure of what he thought he was seeing.

After being replaced by Martha at Milly's bedside, Craig decided to have breakfast back at the Manor before getting some sleep. Even though he had dosed off several times during the night while at the hospital he hadn't had enough. He selected a table in one of the far corners of the dining area which gave him a good view of the entire room. He hadn't been seated long when a male approached. He was pulling an oxygen bottle. Craig noticed that he had clear tubes running from it to his nose. He had a graying beard that reminded Craig of a comedian that always portrayed a drunk. It took a moment, but Craig finally remembered that the comedian's name was Foster Brooks. Seeing that Craig was alone, the man stopped and asked if he could sit at the table. Craig motioned him to a chair. The gentleman was average height, maybe a hundred sixty pounds, Craig noticed. He appeared to be rather unsteady on his feet.

"Thanks," he said as he took the tubes out of his nose and hung them on a hook attached to the handle of the bottle carrier. "My name is Ted, Ted Reese and I just moved in here a couple of days ago."

"I'm Craig Spence. Been here since the place opened. You stuck with that friend of yours wherever you go?"

"Whenever I move around I need it," Ted responded. "When I'm just sitting somewhere I can generally get enough oxygen breathing normally. Yep, it goes where I go."

"How long does a bottle that size last you," Craig asked.

"About four hours," Ted said. Their conversation was interrupted by a server asking for their order.

"I want about a five-eighths glass of milk," Ted began. "Three-quarters glass of orange juice, three eggs scrambled, a piece of wheat toast cut right down the middle, and nothing sweet or fruity on my egg plate." Craig watched as the server, a young female, removed a pitcher of milk from her cart, pick up a glass from the table and dutifully estimate what she thought was about five-eighths. She took a glass that she had in her cart and did the same with the orange juice.

"Can I get you any drinks"? She asked Craig. Totally amazed at what he had witnessed, Craig was speechless.

"Sir," the server said again.

"Sorry," Craig apologized and handed her the glass that was at his setting. "I'll have some tomato juice please, and two eggs over easy with white toast". After pouring his juice she went off to the kitchen.

"Where you from Ted?" Craig asked.

"New Mexico. I was born and raised in a small smelter town called Hurley. I spent most of my adult life in Albuquerque. You?"

Craig went through the story of his life including his boyhood on the ranch, his boxing stint in the Navy, his courting and marriage to Martha, and his years as the Sweetwater County Sheriff. Their food came and they ate in relative silence.

Craig was up and watching a newscast on TV when Martha entered the apartment. She went straight to the living room couch and flopped down.

"Boy, it's been a long day," she said.

"These marathon days aren't for us anymore doll," Craig suggested. "I remember when I could dance all night and go straight to work the next morning. No more. How's the patient?"

"She was awake off and on. They are keeping her sedated. She's not dealing well with the pain. Steve was there when the doctors came. They've decided to do the surgery in the morning, so they are getting her prepped for that. They'll know then if the leg can be saved. They explained to her what the situation was and what they might have to do".

"How did she take it," Craig asked.

"She reached out and took her dad's hand and said, "*It is what it is*" and went back to sleep," Martha explained. "By the way, there was an ambulance out front when I pulled up and I saw that they were taking someone out on a covered gurney. I saw Gretta, one of the managers in the lobby and asked what happened. She said that Rose Carlson, the lady with the spinal problem, had passed away."

"Nice lady she was," Craig recalled. "Before we go down for supper, I'd like you to do me a favor." Craig turned off the TV and picked up the magazine off the coffee table. "Take your finger and cover just half of the man's face in this picture." He turned to the page to the pictures of Thomas Tomblin and his wife. "Just cover the left side of the man's face". Martha covered half of the picture.

"That is a close resemblance to Norman", she said. "Is that what you're thinking?"

"Yep," Craig replied.

"Why would his picture be in this magazine?" Martha was curious.

Craig gave her a summary of the cold case homicide story that he had been reading and the fact that the male body found at the scene was not Tomblin's and that they had not been able to make an identification of it. "If he shows up for supper," Craig continued. "I'd like to take a closer look."

"Once a cop, always a cop?" Martha remarked with some irritation in her voice.

When Craig and Martha entered the dining room for supper, Craig stopped at the entrance and scanned the room. He was amused at the multiple shades of gray of heads bobbling and nodding as table mates conversed with one another. Sure enough, Norman was at a table by himself, and Craig led Martha in that direction.

"May we join you, partner," Craig inquired.

"Sure, I've been wanting to apologize for the way I acted the last time we sat together but I never see ya," Norman replied. Martha took a chair next to Norman and Craig took one directly across the table.

"We've been traveling a lot," Martha explained. We've always wanted to see the country and we're doing it. I don't mean to pry but have you traveled much?"

" I don't mind you asking. I'm in a better mood today. Not much recreational traveling but some. I was a long-haul trucker back in Indiana, so I went through a lot of states but didn't actually see many of them. Never was really interested in moving around just for the fun of it."

"I was probably the same way. If it weren't for Martha I don't think I would have been interested," Craig said as he surveyed the face of the man across from him. The conversation was light throughout the meal and as before, Norman was the first to get up and leave.

"You folks have a good evening," he said as he pushed his chair under the table and left. Martha reached over and took Craig's arm when Norman had gone and said almost in a whisper.

"That is uncanny. There is some resemblance if you block out the part of the face that is scared."

"Could be a coincidence," Craig said. "The name of the police department and the name of the officer working the case are in the magazine story. When this thing is over with Milly, I'll see if Steve might want to check it out and see what the status of the case is and see what he can find out about Thomas Tomblin."

Three hours had passed since they had rolled Milly's bed out at six am on the way to surgery. Steve and Marla had walked, one on each side, to the elevator that would take her down to the operating suites in the lower level of the hospital. They now sat with Craig and Martha in a small waiting room watching a clock on the wall. Mertel had been kind enough to go back and forth to the cafeteria insuring that everyone had coffee or water. She came back at one point with a dozen doughnuts. She knew that everyone had been there since early morning, and no one had had breakfast. As Martha took one of the doughnuts, she looked at the clock and it was half past ten o'clock already.

She took her coffee and doughnut to a vacant chair next to Steve who had been like a yo-yo. He had been up and down, pacing and watching that clock.

"She's in good hands you know," Martha said to him.

"That's not my worry," Steve replied. "What if they take my little girl's leg?"

"They said that they would do everything possible to save the leg," Martha reminded Steve. "Worst case scenario, should it be necessary, your little girl will put her big girl pants on and deal with it."

"I just can't imagine Milly with only one leg," Steve continued.

"Then don't," Martha said sternly. "Think positive. She's in the hands of the best around. I have great confidence that they'll do the best they can for her." Steve got up and began pacing again, Marla left her chair and locked her arm in his and they silently paced together.

At twelve forty-five, Dr. Messenger came in. He was still in his surgeon's hat, his mask dangled to one side of his face, and he was still in his scrubs. There was a sign of fatigue in his eyes.

III

raig Spence wasn't the only person who had become interested in the magazine story regarding the mysterious corpse. Jon "Tito" Pinkerton the one-time manager of a small fitness establishment outside of Evanston Indiana had also read the story. He was now retired but after reading the story Tito remembered that a part-time worker had just not shown up for work about the same time that the fire occurred. He had never reported him missing because the guy was an independent contractor, and they came and went frequently. It was a long time ago and Tito's memory wasn't so good anymore. He could not remember names like he used to. Still, he decided to contact the local police…

After several attempts to speak with someone familiar with the case, Tito met with officer Clarence Stone of the Spencer County Sheriff's Office. Among other duties, Officer Stone was assigned as a cold case investigator. Stone listened intently to Tito's recollections and was informed that independent contractors generally had four or five members for whom they were personal trainers. Stone pressed Tito for a name but no matter how hard he tried, Tito couldn't come up with one.

The name of the fitness operation was Express Gym and it catered to a select clientele. Most of its clients were housewives and female business executives. Its finances were handled by an accounting firm, Evanston Associates, where Officer Stone went to try and get a possible lead as to who the individual once worked for Express as an independent contractor. Since Indiana only required businesses to keep tax and employment records for six years he initially found the staff at Evanston Associates to be of little help.

After several days had passed with no progress on the case, Stone received a call from the manager at Evanston Associates with encouraging news. An envelope had been located that contained time sheets that part-time employees at Express were required to fill out whenever they worked with a client. The time sheets covered the period that Stone was interested in, and he would be welcome to check through them.

Stone found time sheets for three personal trainers that had worked with clients the week prior to and days just before the Tomlin fire. One still worked with clients on and off, another had moved to Florida years ago and the current staff at Express had no knowledge of the other, but Stone noted that the last client he had worked with was Mercy Tomlin, three days before the fire that took her life. The trainer's name was Norman Clayborn. Stone went back to Tito Pinkerton.

"Does Norman Clayborn ring any bells," Stone asked.

"That's it! Tito exclaimed. "That was that guy's name. Why couldn't I remember that?"

"Well, it's been a long time," Stone commented. "Do you remember what he looked like?"

"Yeah," Tito responded. "He was a good-looking guy. Stood a little over six foot, had a full head of jet-black hair, was dark-complected, and had an athletic body build. I now remember that there were rumors that he was quite a ladies' man; in fact, now that I think of it, several of his female clients called asking for him after he disappeared"…

Everyone gathered around Dr. Messenger as he sat himself in one of the waiting room chairs. Steve was the first to speak.

"How'd it go doctor?"

"She came through like a trooper," Messenger replied. "We had intended that the surgery would be exploratory but when we got in we determined that it would be in the best interest of the patient if we did what had to be done immediately. It was necessary to remove some tissue that was suspect but not as much as one might have anticipated under the circumstances. To assist in the bone healing process, Dr. Mason decided to place Milly's leg in a Truelok Fixator. This is a round cage-like device that will keep the bone aligned, prevent any movement and allow the fracture to heal. Milly's enemy in all of this is infection. If we can stave off any infection in that leg, we can save it. Barring any unforeseen complications, I'd estimate that she'll be laid up for a minimum of six months."

"Thank God she won't lose her leg," Steve said with a sigh of relief.

"She's not out of the woods yet," Dr. Messenger cautioned. "We'll need to keep her here two or three weeks so we can keep an eye on the healing process and spot any infection before it can get the jump on us."

"When can we see her?" Marla asked.

"She'll be in recovery for at least an hour and it'll be another hour before she's transferred and situated in her room, so I'd say in a couple of hours. Why don't you folks go get some lunch in the meantime?"

"Good idea," Craig replied. "My stomach thinks something has happened to my throat."

"let's just grab something at the hospital cafeteria," Martha suggested. "That way we won't have to fight traffic."

"How're things at the SO," Craig asked Steve as he was putting salt on his BLT sandwich.

"Really busy," Steve replied. "We're close to capacity at the jail. Lots of people being held pretrial and even more serving thirty- and ninety-day sentences. The jail staff has its hands full."

"I've been meaning to ask," Craig inquired. "How goes things at the hospital now that CPI, the security company that I used to secure people that were detained there, is no longer in business?"

"CPI closed its doors the day you retired," Steve said. "For a short time, we had no one and we had to use deputies. Then one of the guys that had worked for CPI started a small force just to cover the hospital for us, so our guys are back on the road where they belong."

Steve and Craig continued to talk shop as Steve busied himself trying to keep the ingredients of a cheeseburger from slipping out from between the bun and Craig devoured his BLT. When both had finished Craig took the opportunity to mention the magazine story.

"Steve," he said. "I picked up a magazine on one of the trips Martha and I took, and there was a cold case story in it." Craig went on to explain the situation related to the case.

"Sounds like a real mystery, boss," Steve commented. "Didn't know you read that stuff."

"Don't usually," Craig said. "Needed to pass some time at a layover one day and picked up the magazine. Steve, I've got a gut feeling that a guy living at the manor may be connected to that case."

"I've always respected that gut of yours boss. How do you think he's connected?"

"I have a feeling that the male corpse may be a man by the name of Norman Clayborn. All the contact information for the investigator is in the article. I thought maybe if I gave you the magazine, you might be able to see what the status of the case was and what they know about a guy named Norman Clayborn."

"Why do you think the Clayborn fellow is the dead guy's boss?"

"There was a hell of a fire at the place where the bodies were found. There was a male body that is not Thomas Tomblin, the owner of the home, and it has never been identified. There is a man living at the Manor from that area that bears scars on one side of his face and hands from burns. When I lay my thumb over half of the face of Tomblin in the magazine, the right side has an uncanny resemblance to this guy at the manor". Craig took the magazine from his hip pocket, turned to the article, and continued.

"You can barely see it in this picture, but if you look closely you can see a scar in the eyebrow above Tomblin's right eye, see it?"

"Uh-Huh," Steve said.

"The guy at the manor has a scar in the right brow over his right eye," Craig explained. "Coincidence, perhaps but I'm inclined to believe not. The guy goes by the name of Norman Clayborn."

"Okay," Steve said as he moved his head back and forth indicating that he agreed that there was probably something there. " I'll run this by Kevin and have him make contact with the investigator and go from there."

"Hey, you two," Martha wanted their attention. "It's been a while since we've been here. I suggest we let Steve and Marla go to the hospital and the rest of us can stop by and visit later. Milly probably is not up to a bunch of people gawking at her right now anyway."

Milly was awake, groggy, but able to recognize her dad and sister. Her eyes were both blackened, they were black, purple, and a yellowish red now. Her right arm was strapped to her chest and her right leg was elevated, in a sling that was attached to a metal pole and encased in a round contraption that reminded Steve of a small lobster trap.

"You look like a raccoon," Marla said as she approached the bed.

"I feel like road kill," Milly responded softly.

"How ya doing Milly?" Steve asked.

"I really made a mess of things, Huh?" Milly said apologetically.

"Do you remember what happened?" Steve asked.

"Yeah," Milly Said. "I hit a deer and went over the side."

"What were ya doing up there Milly?" Marla asked.

"Looking for a shortcut home," Milly responded. "Considering everything they told me, I guess I'm pretty lucky. They said I have a concussion, I guess that means a cracked skull."

"It could have been worse," Marla said. "But then you've always had a hard head."

"Don't make me laugh," Milly screeched. Marla took Milly's left hand and squeezed lightly.

"Love you girl. You'll be okay. Guess you'll be in here for a while. I'll come to see you every day. Is there anything you need?"

"Nah," Milly said with a sigh. "just wanna sleep." Steve looked at Marla and nodded toward the door. They quietly left the room.

Craig and Martha got back to the Manor just in time for lunch. The dining room was full. Martha spotted a table where there were two empty chairs. The table was occupied by a couple and the woman was in a wheelchair.

"Mind if we set," Craig asked.

"Not at all," the man responded. "I'm Tony Kitchen and my bride is Simone. We're actually just visiting. looking the place over, so having someone to talk to that lives here will surely help."

"Well we've been here since the place opened", Martha said. "I'm Martha Spence and my husband Craig. Where you folks from?"

"Longmont, Colorado," Tony answered. "We have a son that works at a mine west of here and since I'm now retired and Simone is recovering from a stroke, we thought we'd try and move a little closer to family."

"When did you have your stroke?" Martha asked Simon.

"Three months ago," Simone responded. She paused and It was obvious she was struggling to speak.

"Sometimes –," she continued. "words are hard – but it's - better. I was – standing by my kitchen sink- washing dishes -and that's where Tony--- found me, just - standing there." Martha admired Simone for her courage and determination to master her situation.

"She has lost the use of her left side," Tony advised. "A month ago she couldn't speak at all, so we are blessed."

"What did you do before you retired," Craig asked Tony.

"I was the Band Master at the high school where we lived. Spent twenty-two years there. I would have continued there but Simone needed me."

"Well, welcome to Green River, Wyoming," Martha said. "We were both born and raised here, and we really didn't want to live any place else. Craig was Sheriff of this county for twenty years and when he retired we looked at other places, but when this place opened we moved in."

"How did you manage twenty years," Tony asked. "There's no way a guy would last in that job that long in Colorado."

"Guess nobody else wanted the job," Craig replied, and everyone chuckled.

The server was standing by to take their order, so the conversation was limited thereafter. After lunch, they heard someone yell as they entered the elevator that would take them to the second floor.

"Hold the door! Hold the door"! It was Mertel calling out as she ran toward them. Once on the elevator, she showed Craig a package that she held.

"The pictures," she said. "I just got back from picking up the pictures that we took the other day. Most of them are gorgeous. I'll show you when we get upstairs if you've got a minute."

"I don't know about Craig, but I want to see them," Martha said as they exited the elevator and Craig hurried across the hall to open the apartment door. "Come on in."

As soon as Steve got back to his office at the County Detention Center he pulled out the magazine that Craig Spence had given him. He perused the story again and made note of the investigator's name and contact details on his desk pad. He decided to follow up himself and he made a phone call.

The dispatcher at the Spencer County Sheriff's office advised Steve that Sargent Stone was on a call, but she would advise him when he checked back in. She took Steve's phone number and he put the magazine in his desk drawer. After some time had passed he got a call.

"This is Steve Lolly," he answered.

"Sargent Stone of the Spencer County Sheriff's Office sir. I understand you wished to speak to me."

"Yeh Sargent Stone," Steve responded. "I suppose the dispatcher told you that I am the Sheriff of Sweetwater County in Wyoming?"

"Yes sir," Stone responded. "Don't think I've ever gotten a call from Wyoming, especially not from a sheriff."

"Don't think I've ever made a call to Indiana either," Steve said, and they had a light moment. "I have here a magazine, a True Detective magazine, in which there is a story about a cold case from about ten years ago. It tells of a fire and two homicides. According to the story, one of the victims has never been identified."

"That's correct sheriff, and I've been dogging this case ever since. A male victim found at the scene was not the owner of the home and he disappeared into thin air. There has never been a trace of him. I surmise that he might be the perpetrator, but I haven't been able to locate him, and all leads have long dried up."

"Tell me, Sargent," Steve picked up the conversation. "What do you know about a fellow by the name of Norman Clayborn?"

"Norman Clayborn was a physical therapist who worked as a personal trainer at a small health establishment. He wasn't an employee, but he had several clients that he worked with."

"Was either of his clients one of the Tomblin people?" Steve asked.

"As I recall, Mrs. Tomblin was a client of his," Stone replied.

"What happened to Clayborn?" Steve asked.

"From what I was told he just didn't show up one day and he hasn't been seen since. What are you getting at Sheriff?" Stone seemed curious.

"I'm getting there," Steve said. "But tell me, I understand that the corpse of that male person was pretty well consumed by the fire, did anyone ever check the dental work against that of Norman Clayborn?"

"Not that I'm aware of sir, there never seemed to be any connection."

"Well, there's a probability that he never had any dental work done there anyway," Steve surmised. "Tell me what Norman looked like if you know."

"A guy that was a manager of the place where Norman worked told me that Clayborn had an athletic physique, was dark skinned with a full head of dark hair," Stone described. "You want to tell me what you're getting at sheriff?"

"Yeh Sargent Stone", Steve said. "The gentleman that was sheriff before me lives in a senior living place. He read the story about the fire and the homicides in a magazine and compared the picture of Thomas Tomblin to a man currently living at the senior living manor. He bears the scars from being burned on one side of his face, but he also bares a scar over his right eye that matches one visible in the picture of Tomblin in the magazine. Also, the description you just gave of Clayborn in no way matches the guy in the manner. Do you have a description of Tomblin"?

"All I know about him is that he was a long-haul truck driver and heavy set", Stone related. "That's about all I know beside the picture we got off a driver's license found at the crime scene and a picture that the

Amador Distributers had on file. That's whom he drove for. He showed up for work the morning of the fire, but his truck was being worked on. He went back home and was never heard from again".

"What do you think Sargent?" Steve asked. "Think you have enough to do some more checking?"

"You've got me all excited, Sheriff," Stone said. "This is the best lead I've had in years."

It had been many months since Detective Stone had had any incentive to delve into the cold case. He felt that he needed to refresh his memory regarding the details, so he revisited the evidence room at the sheriff's department. It was a large room, most of which was protected by wire mesh behind which were rows of racks filled with boxes, large envelopes, paper bags, and all types of items imaginable. Inside this cage, the sergeant on duty looked like he had been hit by a truck, Stone thought. His right arm was in a cast, he had one of those styrofoam braces around his neck and he used a crutch under his left arm.

"What the hell happened to you sarge?" Stone asked.

"You remember that freak snowstorm we had a week or so ago?" The sergeant began. "Well, I came out that morning to get in my car, opened the car door and my feet went out from under me. Must have tried to catch myself because I broke the arm, pulled something in my neck and twisted my left knee. What can I do for you detective?"

"I need to check out the evidence box for case number 72000143-14", Stone advised. The sergeant wrote the number down on a post-it and hobbled over to the door that would allow entrance to where the evidence was secured.

"You're gonna have to look through it at that table over by the wall anyway," the sergeant said. So I'll open the security door and you can go with me back in the dungeon- that's what we call that part of the place where all the old cases are kept- once we find it you'll have to dig it out for me."

Together they walked between two rows of racks to the very back of the room. The dungeon was a step down from the main floor and the walls were lined with wooden cabinets, each tagged with a number, starting with the number 60 and progressing upward through the sixty's and seventy's. At cabinet numbered seventy-two, they stopped, and the sergeant took a set of keys from his pocket and unlocked the cabinet door. The contents of the cabinet were a medium-sized cardboard box and a large manila envelope. Detective Stone gathered them up and took them to the designated review area. He checked the contents of the box first.

A large brown paper bag contained some fragments of burned bed clothes, clear plastic envelopes with a wallet that had been partially burned. It contained a discolored Indiana driver's license that had been issued to Thomas Tomblin. The date and license number were unreadable. Miraculously, several credit cards had survived the fire. A set of keys were in the same envelope. He remembered that the keys were to a Chevy Silverado, parked in front of the residence, which belonged to Thomas Tomblin. There was a fat file containing all the police and forensic reports pertaining to the case. Stone perused the reports to refresh his knowledge of the case and to see if anything jumped out at him at this late date- Nothing did.

The large manila envelope contained photographs of the crime scene including the locations of the human remains in the burned residence, a picture of a disfigured gas can, a photograph of what remained of what appeared to be a kitchen butcher knife and photographs taken by the coroner of the teeth from each of the remains.

"Sergeant," he called out and the attendant hobbled over. "I need to check out a couple of these photographs."

"Sorry detective," the attendant shook his head. "Can't let you do that. There is a copy machine over in the corner though, I can make copies for you if that'll work."

"That'll work," Stone said and handed over the photos of the teeth from the unidentified male. Now that he had a name to work with he would canvass the dental establishments in town to see if he could come up with a match.

Stone identified fifteen dental providers in and around Evanston. He made contact with the dentist or managers whenever his efforts at current investigations found him in their locations. It took several weeks for him to contact them all asking if their records for the year nineteen seventy-two and years prior reflected a patient by the name of Norman Clayborn. A response finally came from a local Endodontic Specialist to the Spencer County Sheriff's Office. The dispatcher advised Stone that he was to return a call and ask for Dr. Mark. Once back in his office, he dialed the number he'd been given. The phone rang several times before it was answered.

"Dr. Mark Caster Dental services, this is Christine may I help you?" *The voice was light and pleasant* Stone thought.

"This is Detective Stone with the Spencer County Sheriff's Office," Stone responded. "I'd like to speak to Dr. Mark please."

"He's with a patient at the moment detective," Christine advised. "Can I have him call you in a few?"

"Sure," Stone replied, and he gave Christine the number to his direct line. While he waited he took out the envelope that had the photos of the crime scene of the Tomblin case. In a little over fifteen minutes the phone rang, and Stone answered.

"Detective Stone," he answered.

"This is Dr. Mark, I believe you were interested in knowing if a person had been one of my patients," the voice sort of a baritone-monotone.

"Yes sir," Stone responded. "I was interested in Norman Clayborn."

"Well, a man by that name was a patient of mine back in early seventy-two. Because of privacy restrictions that's about all I can tell you."

"Dr. Mark," Stone spoke up in his best authoritative voice. "I have reason to believe that Norman Clayborn may be dead. I have in my possession copies of photographs showing the teeth- that was all that was left of remains- that for ten years have not been identified. I'd like to have you look at these photographs and see if there might be a match".

"Oh, I see," Dr. Mark remarked. "If you'd care to drop the pictures by I'd be glad to take a look. We close at five this evening".

"Thank you, sir, " Stone said, a little excitement in his voice. "I'll be by shortly."

Stone checked the contents of the envelope to make sure the photos he wanted to show to the dentist were indeed still there. He checked his watch; it was three o'clock in the afternoon. Depending on traffic it would take about twenty minutes to get to Dr. Mark's office. He advised dispatch of his intentions and was on his way.

Dr. Mark had an X-ray view of an upper and lower jaw on a lightbox when Stone arrived at his office. He laid out the photos that Stone brought and visually compared them to those in the box. Dr. Mark explained what he saw.

"What you see here is an X-ray of the upper and lower images of the teeth of a patient by the name of Norman Clayborn. Using the universal method of numbering, we start with the upper arch on the right side and count from one through sixteen. Then we start on the lower arch on the left side in the rear and count sixteen through thirty-two. The X-ray shows that Mr. Clayborn had the first molar, number fourteen, missing and number four has a gold cap. It also shows that number thirty has what appears to be a temporary filling and an open canal. Based on Mr. Clayborn's records we were in the process of doing a root canal on number thirty, but he never returned to have it completed." Dr. Mark then took a pencil and showed Stone the comparisons on the photos and continued. "I can't see the open canals on number thirty on these photos but what I do see would leave me to believe that they are representative of what I see in the X-ray images. I'd say with confidence that your dead man is Mr. Clayborn."

"Can I get a copy of those X-rays," Stone asked.

"No," Dr. Mark replied. "Not without a court order. I will, however, provide you with a written statement confirming that I have made a comparison and what my findings are."

"If you don't mind sir, I'll wait for it," Stone said…

IV

Tom Tomblin went to work at The Amador Distributors on that fateful morning expecting to drive a load of produce to the east coast. The trip would encompass a three-day turnaround. He was a heavy smoker, so he had stopped at a convenience store and purchased a carton of cigarettes. Upon arrival at the terminal, he found the rig in the maintenance building. He was told that the refrigeration unit was not operating properly. The repair parts would be overnighted. That meant that he would have another whole day that he could spend at home with his wife Mercy.

He got back into his beige-colored Silverado pickup, joyful that he wouldn't have to hit the road until the next day. His house was across town, and the trip took him about thirty-five minutes to get there. His home sat on a two-acre plot in a development that was underway. There were few homes there and they were far apart from each other. As his house came into view he noticed a vehicle parked in the driveway. As he approached he noticed that it was a black Ford Two-Fifty with large off-road type tires and a light bar across the cab. It wasn't one that he recognized.

Tom pulled his truck along the curb in front of the house and walked up the drive, and around to the back door of the residence. He entered the kitchen and walked through the dining room. He could hear voices. He stopped and listened. The voices were coming from the bedroom. The blood began to pound in his head, he could feel the heat move up from his chest, the vessels in his neck expanding to the point that they hurt. He went back to the kitchen and got a butcher knife from the cabinet drawer.

Slowly he made his way through the dining room, down the long hallway toward the bedroom. The shades were closed but he could see the silhouette of his wife, Mercy, over someone on the bed. Her back was to him. He lost it. He lounged into the room, and he could hear himself screaming as he stabbed and stabbed again at the back of Mercy. Her screams did nothing to diminish his rage. The person below her scrambled from the bed but Tom slashed out with the knife as he screamed obscenities. The man stumbled and Tom jumped on him cursing and stabbing until there was no movement.

He stood up, panting and whimpering. Blood was everywhere; on the bed, the floor, and on him. He stripped off his clothes and left them at the foot of the bed. The shower, he made his way to the shower and stood under the pulsating water. His mind began to clear, Dear God, what have I done, he thought. He dried and got clean clothes from his closet. He knew now that he had to cover what he'd done.

Tom went to the shed out back of the house and got a five-gallon gas can. He had used the gas to fill his riding mower when he cut the grass on the two acres. It was full. Back in the house, he poured the gasoline on the bed, on Mercy, on the floor, and the body of the dead guy, on his bloody clothes, and out into the hall. He then noticed the guy's clothes on a chair. He put the can down and went through the pockets of the pants. He found a wallet and he replaced it with his own. He also found a set of car keys and put them in his pocket and left the keys to his Silverado in their place. He stood for a moment and surveyed the room, before reaching into his pocket and taking out a cigarette lighter.

There was an explosion, and he ran down the hall out the back door and fell to the ground. His face stung and his hands were stinging too. He made his way to the black Ford, got it started, and drove away.

He could see the flames and smoke consuming the house as he left. The jacket he was wearing was made of nylon and he could smell the material that had been melted by the fire.

He made his way to US Route Thirty and headed toward Ft. Wayne. The burns on his hands and face were becoming excruciating. He gritted his teeth and kept driving. After about an hour the pain finally took its toll, and he passed out. The truck veered into the median of the highway coming to rest in a culvert where the underside of the engine compartment burst into flames.

A passing trucker witnessed the accident and stopped to help. With the truck's fire extinguisher in hand, he reached the wreck just as the flames were beginning to lap at the interior of the vehicle. Tom was lying prone on the seat. The trucker pulled Tom out onto the ground, away from the burning truck, and used the fire extinguisher from his truck to spray on Tom.

Tom awoke in a hospital in Ft. Wayne. His head was bandaged and there was an opening so he could see out of his right eye. His hands were bandaged too. The nurses all referred to him as Mr. Clayborn and the police officer that came to take a report on the accident assumed that the burns were the result of the accident. After several days of treatment, he was able to look through the wallet he'd taken from the pants at the house in Evanston. There were two credit cards, one Visa and one with Coastal Finance, a debit card for an account at Evanston National: an insurance card with Colonial Insurance Company, and three hundred thirty dollars in cash.

Using the hospital phone at his bedside, Thomas called the customer service numbers on each of the cards to verify the balances. He was amazed at the amount of money that Clayborn had access to and the amount of cash in a checking account at Evanston National.

When he was released from the hospital he provided them with the information on the insurance card. At a local used car dealership, he purchased a used Chevy pickup with the Coastal Finance card and drove to Shreveport, Louisiana.

For several years he drove a delivery truck for a seafood distributor. The company was eventually purchased by a large corporation and when they initiated background checks on all of the old company's employees, paranoia set in with Tomblin and he hit the road again. After taking refuge in several locations across the country for some periods of time, he finally ended up in Green River, Wyoming, and decided to settle in at the Senior Living facility, He met the minimum residency age of fifty-five. He figured he'd just hang out in the senior living facility until his money was about to run out…

Steve was in his office reviewing reports from the previous day when Heather, the receptionist buzzed his phone.

"Yes Heather," he answered.

"Sheriff, I have Detective Stone on the phone," she began. "He says he's with a department in Indiana and he needs to talk with you."

"Yes," Steve responded. "Patch him through Heather." The phone rang and Steve picked up.

"Detective Stone, this is Sheriff Lolly," he said.

"Good day to you Sheriff," Stone said in greeting. "I've been doing some follow-up work based on the information we discussed on our last phone call several weeks ago."

"Uh-huh, and what were you able to find out?" Steve asked.

"I found a dentist that had done some work on Clayborn's mouth," Stone responded. " I took photographs that the coroner had taken of the teeth belonging to the corpse that we couldn't identify over to that dentist and guess what? He was able to get a match on his dental records of Clayborn. The remains found at the scene of the Tomblin house fire I believe was of Norman Clayborn."

"And you believe the individual living at the Manor is---?" Steve posed a question.

"To be anyone other than Tom Tomblin would be a coincidence beyond belief," Stone remarked.

" So what's your plan?" Steve asked.

"Don't know yet," Detective Stone responded. "I'll have to run all of this by my people and see how we handle it. I appreciate all your help sir, and as soon as we work out the details you'll be hearing from us. In the meantime, I'd appreciate you keeping an eye on that guy."

"Will do detective," Steve assured. "Looking forward to hearing from you."

As they often did, Craig, Martha, and Mertel sat together for the evening meal in the dining room. As they seated themselves servers were flitting about taking orders and delivering food to the tables. When one stopped at their table Craig spoke to the server.

"What are we having tonight," he asked. Liver and onions was the response.

"Yuk!" Mertel exclaimed. "I never was able to get it past my lips."

"Oh come on," Craig consoled. "It's not that bad. Good for your gullet."

"My gullet is not hungry," Mertel retorted.

"Stop it you two", Martha admonished. Turning to the server she asked. "Is there an alternate by chance?" Stuffed green peppers were the response.

"I'll have that," Mertel happily requested. Craig and Martha settled for the liver.

While they were dining Steve Lolly entered the room. He was in his uniform which was always meticulously adorned. As he strode from the entrance, past the dinners to where Craig was sitting he attracted much attention, especially from Norman. He was sitting alone across the room. Steve stopped at Craig's table, got down on one knee, and spoke softly into Craig's ear. While listening to Steve, Craig turned his head slightly.

To Norman, Craig appeared to be looking at him and he began to be paranoid. He remembered that Craig was an ex-sheriff, and he began to go over in his mind the conversations he'd had with him. *Why would they be talking about him?* He thought. *They couldn't possibly know anything about him.* He thought. *He surely never said anything that would give them a clue.* He thought. He no longer had an appetite; his stomach was knotting up; He decided food was no longer appealing. As he was leaving the room he was sure they were watching him…

When Steve met Craig in the Manor dining room he proceeded to let him know what he had found out about Norman.

"That gut of yours hasn't lost a beat as time has passed," Steve began. "I've been in contact with the detective handling the case we read about in that magazine. They've been able to identify the remains of that male by matching the teeth found at the scene with dental records and they got a match. They think the dead guy was Norman Clayborn."

"So this guy is probably Tom Tomblin," Craig surmised as he glanced at Norman across the room. "Have they asked that you make an arrest?" Craig asked.

"Not yet," Steve responded. "When they produce a plan they'll get back to me. Just thought you'd like to know that your premonition was right on. They watched as Norman or Tom Tomblin left the room.

"I was just minding my own business, trying to pass away some time," Craig said. " It was kinda neat to have been able to connect the dots though."

It was Saturday and Craig, in his stocking feet and a jumpsuit was lounging in his favorite chair watching college football. Martha too, was comfortable in a pair of slippers and a house coat thumbing through magazines that had come in the mail, and she would eventually just throw them away. There was a knock at the door. Martha walked over to answer it.

"Who is it?" Craig heard her say.

"It's Marla," came a reply, and Martha considering her family hurriedly unlocked the door. Craig heard Martha shout.

"Oh my God, look who's here"! Craig left his chair and moved to the door. There was Marla and behind her was Milly, on crutches with a big black boot on that right leg, Grinning from ear to ear.

"Hey Doll," Craig said. "When'd cha get out?"

"They kicked me out yesterday," Milly responded. "Said I was just taking up space and I could go home."

"It's so good to see you up and about," Martha said as she carefully gave Milly a hug. "Come on in and sit."

"I'll bet your dad is glad to have you home," Craig commented.

"Yeah," Milly answered. "He spent so much time at the hospital that it was like a satellite office for him. I kept telling him, Dad I'm okay, they're taking good care of me, but he insisted on spending a couple of hours every day with me. It was cool."

"What did they ever do with your car?" Craig inquired.

"The insurance company totaled it," Marla answered. "They gave us enough money to pay it off, so now we're looking to see what to replace it with."

"It will be a while before I can drive again so we have plenty of time," Milly interjected.

"What about your Job?" Martha asked.

"They said that when I'm ready to come back, my job would be there," Milly advised.

"The leg, what about the leg?" Martha wondered. "is it healing all right?"

"The bone healed nicely", Milly began. "The incision from the surgery was the last thing closed up and it's still healing inside. Some of the muscle is gone so it's weak. I go to rehab three times a week to strengthen it."

"And the shoulder?" Craig asked.

"Sore, but good," Milly said.

"You're one lucky girl," Martha said.

"Sure wasn't worth a shortcut," Milly responded.

The girls spent most of the day visiting with Martha and Craig, Marla engaging Martha in discussing her future plans and Milly watching football with Craig.

Norman now spent most days in his one-bedroom apartment, only leaving to eat one meal a day in the Manor dining room. He alternated, some days eating breakfast, other days eating lunch or supper. Something was up. Was it all just in his head? Was he getting overly paranoid? Should he make plans to make another move? Norman spent much of his time isolated in his apartment going over events in his life since being on the run. He especially thought of the time spent in Louisiana and his friend Janice Moir…

Janice was a portly woman who always wore her hair in a role that hung on one side of her head and over her left shoulder. Whenever she was being thoughtful she would put her hair in her mouth and chew on it. Janice owned a small restaurant and a boarding house along one of the lagoons near where Norman worked, and he rented a room from her. He ate all his meals there, even when he'd break for lunch. She had taken a liking to Norman, and they became close friends, spending lots of time sitting along the docks and levies, visiting and just enjoying one another's company. Janice was a religious woman who often invited Norman to go with her to church, but he always begged off. Sometime before the business Norman worked for was bought out, their friendship took a more serious turn. They were sitting outside the restaurant enjoying the sun and watching shrimp boats come and go when Janice caught him by surprise.

"You know Norman", she began. "I know you now, four-maybe five years, but I really don't know about you. I know you come from Indiana-you never talk about family, what you do in Indiana, why you come here- nothing. Why you don't talk about these things?"

"You never asked," Norman replied.

"So, now I ask," Janice said. "What about your Mom'N'Em?" (Immediate Family).

"My parents died years ago when I was still in High School," Norman said. "I was an only child, no siblings. I was raised by my Grandmother, she's gone now too."

"What kinda work do you do back there in Indiana?" Janice asked.

"Early on I bussed tables in a restaurant," Norman replied. "The dad of a friend of mine had a trucking service and he taught me to drive trucks. So that's what I did most of my adult life, just like I'm doing now."

"You never marry?" Janice continued to question him. After a long pause, Norman answered.

"I was married once," he said but made no further comment.

"Well, what happened to her, your wife I mean?" Janice was chewing on her hair as she waited for Norman to answer. As if he was talking to himself, without giving it a thought Norman spoke softly.

"I killed her," he said. There was a loud silence. *It seemed to Norman that the whole world had stopped. For years he had shut it out of his mind and not said those words to anyone, and even now, thinking about what had taken place back then was the cause of some emotion.*

Janice stopped breathing when she heard what Norman said. She fixed her eyes on his face and he was off in some far-off place. Slowly, she began to exhale, and she laid a hand on Norman's arm.

"Norman," she spoke softly. "Why you do that? Why do you kill your wife?"

Norman turned his head and looked into Janice's eyes. Her touch had brought him out of the trance that he had gone into, and he thought to himself: *What have I done? Why did I tell her?* After what seemed to Janice a long time, Norman spoke.

"I caught her cheating with a man," he told her. "I don't know what happened to me. I saw red. When I realized what I'd done to them I covered it up."

"You run, huh Norman?" It was more of a statement than a question that Janice said. "You run and come to this place."

"Yeh," He acknowledged.

"Your face and your hands, how you get them scars?" Janice asked.

"When I realized what I'd done," Norman began. "I knew I had to cover it up, so I poured gasoline over everything. I waited too long to light it up. Fumes built up and when I flicked the lighter, BOOM-the whole room lit up. It burned me."

"All these years, you running; looking over your shoulder, remembering what happened and what you have done," Janice said as if summing up Norman's situation.

"Boo," using that word of endearment she addressed him. "you been trying to run from yourself. Where you go, that thing goes with you. You cain't run far enough"…

During the days that followed the scene in the dining room, where the uniformed officer was talking to Craig Spence and he felt they were talking about him, he couldn't get Janice's words out of his head. *"you been trying to run from yourself- you cain't run far enough."* He began to make a serious assessment of his life since he hurt Mercy, the love of his life, he trusted her, and she betrayed him. All through the many years thereafter he couldn't let himself be vulnerable. He was close to no one except Janice, and she was like a sister that he'd never had. He'd grown old alone, with no place to call home, no future without being hunted. Like a rabbit, always ready to run for cover.

aving seen all the places on her bucket list, Martha settled in to experience the benefits and pleasures of living in a senior living facility. She found that there was always something to do. Teams were formed to play games: balloon volleyball and beanbag baseball; watching old movies or listening to musicians that the Manor's activity director would arrange to come in.

She learned to play Farkel, a card game she had never heard of before, and Nickels, a game in which you roll dice. If you had the number rolled on your sheet you placed a nickel on it. Whoever covered all the numbers on their sheet first would win the game and take all the nickels that other players had on their sheets.

Every day Martha engaged in some activity that had been planned by the activities director of the Senior Manor at Green River. She really enjoyed the adult coloring sessions and Jewelry making. Periodically she and Craig joined others on bus trips to Salt Lake City, Utah, or Casper and Cheyenne to eat at popular restaurants or attend some sporting event.

The most rewarding thing for Martha was making new friends such as Margo Sanchez. Margo was a sixty-eight-year-old, petite Hispanic lady from Cortez, New Mexico. She wore her hair in long braids that extended down her back to her waist, but on the sides of her head, her hair was rolled in such a way that her olive-colored face was encased. She had large dark eyes, and they were accented by heavy black eyebrows.

Margo had come to Wyoming a few years earlier to visit her son who was in the Air Force and stationed at Warren Air Force Base in Cheyenne. While visiting she saw a posting in the local paper for a Spanish-speaking interpreter at the District Court in Green River, Wyoming. Her son had driven her down for an interview. She learned there was a large Basque ethnic group of people who worked for the large sheep ranches in Wyoming. Even though Euskara is the main language of the Basque, and it is linguistically distinct from any other language, Spanish was secondary. She got the job. She would stand with a defendant, tell him in Spanish what was transpiring, and when he was required to answer he would speak to her in Spanish, and she would convey his answer in English.

It was a fun job, but on one of those typical Wyoming wintery days, when snow and ice were on the ground, she stepped out of her car in the courthouse parking lot, slipped-fell, and broke her hip. After going through surgery and rehab she could no longer stand for long periods of time, so she gave up her dream job. On top of that, her son was transferred to Saudi Arabia. When his tour there was completed he would return to his unit at Warren, so she decided to move into the Manor until he returned.

Martha and Margo teamed up as Canasta partners on Tuesday and Thursday afternoons and played Farkel together on Tuesday and Friday evenings. On Wednesday afternoon, Martha joined ten other women in a jewelry-making class and she sat next to Ingeborg (Inge for short) Van Heusen, a very opinionated seventyish lady from Europe. She had been married to a retired Air Force pilot for fifty-seven years. They had purchased a home in Casper, Wyoming, and lived there until he passed on as a result of Prostate Cancer. She sold the home and moved into the Manor. Inge used a walker and was on oxygen whenever she was moving about. There was always a small canister in a bag on the front of her walker and clear plastic tubing from it to her nose. Martha found her to be very bossy, but she had a great eye for matching colors and designing necklaces and earrings. She had a full head of white hair and was big-boned like Martha remembered women she had seen in the farm country in Germany.

Craig emersed himself in his new hobby, Photography. He traveled around the county to small towns and Indian reservations photographing old buildings, old mining digs, tourist locations, and of course any wildlife that he might come across. The local mercantile store in Green River allowed him to display postcards for sale that he had made from his pictures.

Three weeks after Steve Lolly had spoken to Detective Stone a brown envelope was delivered by United Parcel Service. The UPS driver allowed Heather to sign for it and she delivered the envelope to Steve. It was a letter from the Sheriff of Spencer County in Indiana summarizing the investigation and detailing evidence developed that leads him to believe that the perpetrator of the specific crimes committed, Tom Tomblin/aka Norman Clayborn, is located in the jurisdiction of Sweetwater County Sheriff and requesting assistance in apprehending the person named. The letter went on to state where Tom Tomblin was believed to be living and it was attached to an arrest warrant.

It was a little after eight pm when Steve knocked on Craig's apartment door. Martha was the one who answered.

"Well hello Steve," she said. "What's wrong that you're out so late?"

"Hey Martha," Steve responded. "Nothing's wrong, I need to talk with the boss man, and I thought it would be best to come when there wouldn't be a lot of people moving around."

"Well, come on in. He's watching the TV with his eyes closed," Martha said, and they both laughed. "Steve's here to see you, Craig," she called out.

"Steve's welcome anytime," Craig responded. " What did I do to deserve a visit from such a busy man as you? Is something wrong?"

"No Sir," Steve assured. "I just received the arrest warrant from the Sheriff in Indiana, and I could use your help."

"How so son?" Craig inquired. "You know I'll do what I can to be of help."

"I want to do this as quickly as I can," Steve began. "I don't want to storm this place and surprise management and at the same time I don't want to put out any information to anyone who will leak it before we can surprise our target."

"So where do I come in?" Craig asked.

"I'm planning to make the arrest tomorrow night," Steve said. "We'll contact Tom Tomblin at eleven o'clock PM. Your management here lives on-site. I'd appreciate it if at ten thirty PM, you contacted the management team and advised them of what's happening so that the front doors will be unlocked. We'll be at the doors at ten forty-five PM."

"I think your timing will be perfect. All of the residents will be bedded down by ten PM or a little after," Craig surmised. "Just a minute and I'll tell you exactly where his apartment is." As he spoke Craig went to the kitchen and removed a roster from the side of the refrigerator. He's in this wing on the third floor, apartment number 323".

"May I have that sheet", Steve asked, and Craig handed it to him. "I don't plan to be kicking any doors in, so I would appreciate someone from management standing by up there with a key to the apartment."

"I'll let em know when I contact them," Craig said.

"Great," Steve said with some relief. "In case things don't work out as planned with management, you'll have fifteen minutes to let us know by phone. Just call dispatch."

"I'm proud of ya Steve," Craig said as he patted Steve on the back.

"Had a good teacher," Steve responded.

The next morning Steve held a briefing at the detention center. Instead of holding them in his office as Craig did many times unless guests were invited, Steve had a nice classroom arrangement in the new facility. After getting a report from all of his supervisors, he delved into the planning for the night's apprehension.

"A fugitive out of Indiana is currently living in our jurisdiction and we have been requested to apprehend him and arrange to return him to that state," Steve began. "I need three volunteers to help me accomplish the arrest."

"I can get a couple of deputies to do this," Kevin spoke up. He was now the Chief Deputy since Steve had taken over the duties of Sheriff.

"OK," Steve said. "The person is living on the third floor of the Senior Manor of Green River. That's the same place Sheriff Spence is living now. In fact, he is going to alert management of the situation and make sure that there's a key available in case he won't open the door. The building has a long metal walkway the length of the wing on the back side," Steve continued. "There is a stairway at each end of the walkway. Each apartment has a door through which the walkway can be accessed. I want a deputy stationed outside, on the ground, in case he rabbits on us. I want two deputies with me when we make entry."

"What time are we going to do this?" Kevin asked and Steve continued laying out his plan.

"We'll be at the front doors of the Manor at ten forty-five tonight. Someone from Management will be there to open the doors for us. It is expected that there will be little or no traffic by the residents at that time."

"What if?" Kevin asked. "What if for some reason there are people about?"

"We'll go about our business," Seve responded. "We'll take the elevator from the lobby to the third floor. When we get off we'll flip the switch that will disable the elevator preventing anyone from getting to the third floor. There is a stairway, but I'm not too concerned about it being used by people that live there. If someone does, we'll direct management to send them back the way they came."

Steve paused, to see if Kevin had any further questions, then he continued. "We'll be at the door of the apartment at eleven pm. With a deputy posted on each side, I'll take the key from the person from management and open the door. We will not, I repeat. We will not kick the door in."

"What if he rabbits?" Kevin asked.

"If he rabbits the deputy posted below will let us know by radio," Steve replied. "We'll follow him onto the walkway and pin him between us, however, I plan to be in the room before he has any idea of what's happening. It's a one-bedroom apartment so there's a likely hood that we will be blocking any escape route. Once we have him in custody we'll bring him back here and hold him until arrangements can be made to get him back to Indiana."

"What if there's gunplay?" Kevin asked.

"I have no reason to believe that this guy is dangerous, and I plan for us to be on him before he has a chance to arm himself, but if it comes to that we may have to send him to Indiana in a body bag."

"OK Steve," Kevin said. "Got it. We'll meet you at the front doors at ten forty-five."

As planned, Steve, Kevin, and the deputies met at the Manor doors at ten forty-five as planned and the doors were opened by Gretta, one of the managers that lived on site. Craig was also standing by and along with Gretta accompanied the officers to the elevator. Once on the third floor, Gretta disabled the elevator as Steve had instructed her on the way up. At door number 323 Steve took the key from Gretta, made sure the deputies were positioned in their proper places, and motioned Craig and Gretta to stand back out of the way.

Very slowly and quietly he inserted the key into the door lock. Everyone assumed a crotched stance and when Steve pushed the door open, rushed into the room. The only light was from a window on the far wall of the living room. They could barely make out the silhouettes of each other. Each of the deputies had flashlights and they used them to survey the room. There was a faint, putrid odor in the air, everyone recognized the smell and turned their attention to the closed door that led to the bedroom.

Again in a crouched stance, Steve opened the door and his flashlight illuminated a gruesome scene. Someone found a light switch and turned the ceiling light on. Tom Tomblin was sitting in bed with a plastic bag over his head. Kevin was the first to speak.

"Well, I guess he made the decision about how he'd go back."

"I knew we'd find a dead man when that smell hit us out in the living room," Steve said. "Once you've smelled death you never forget it. From the looks of him and the faint odor, I'd estimate he's been dead three maybe four days. Let's get out of here and close the door or we'll never get the odor out of our clothes. Kevin, get ahold of the coroner's office so they can get him."

When all were out, Steve locked the door to the apartment. He approached Craig and Gretta who were still waiting for some distance from room 323. Craig inquired.

"Well, wasn't he there?"

"He was there," Steve replied. "Looks like he was tired of running. Looks like he decided to take his own life."

"OH MY'! Gretta exclaimed. I'll need to call the police department."

"That won't be necessary miss," Steve said. "We take care of everything. We'll try and get the body out of there as soon as practical, and we'll also give you the contact information for a professional cleaning team that you'll need to sanitize that apartment."

"How'd he do it", Craig asked as they started down in the elevator.

"There was a plastic bag over his head", Steve answered. "Strange though, didn't appear to be any type of struggling or thrashing or anything. He's just sitting up straight in the bed"….

"Boo, you been *trying to run from yourself. Where you go, that thing goes with you. You cain't run far enough".* Those words dominated Tomblin's thoughts as he tried to decide what he should do. He toyed with the idea of just giving himself up. The thought of spending the rest of his days in some prison was terrifying. He tried to convince himself that he was being overly concerned, but that didn't work. *He* knew something was up. Somehow they knew about him.

"Boo, you been trying to run from yourself. Where you go, that thing goes with you. You cain't run far enough". Janice's voice was always in his head. He made a decision.

When he was driving a long Haul back in Indiana, the maintenance guys always filled his tires with dry nitrogen. They said that the loss of tire pressure because of valve leaks or tire seal leaks would be reduced because the molecules of nitrogen were heavier than air and tire pressure wouldn't fluctuate. That's why guys that drive race cars use it. They also told him that using nitrogen in a confined place could be dangerous because breathing it in would cause a person to suffocate.

In the phone book, he found a tire company that catered to racing car drivers. He drove over and engaged the manager in conversation about his experiences driving a truck cross country and that he was going to be driving back east and wanted to have his tires filled with nitrogen. Although the Manager told him that it was a waste of money to fill passenger car tires with gas, Tom insisted and got his tires filled. While that was being done he walked across the street to a Kum and Go convenience store and bought a package of small plastic trash bags with draw ribbons. Back in the Manor parking lot, Tom unscrewed one of the tire valve cores and allowed the gas to flow into a plastic bag. When he thought he had enough he twisted the open end of the bag to keep the gas from escaping....

VI

raig had begun to enjoy an early morning walk along the Green River which flowed passed the Manor. The county parks people had constructed a viewing platform where it turned to enter the canyon to the south. It was now Spring, and the morning air was still a little brisk, but the sunrise was spectacular. As he stood on the platform this morning he watched small fish jumping, their bodies glistening in the sunlight as they cleared the river's ripples. *There must be a larger fish looking for breakfast*, he thought.

As he began his trek back to the Manor, he saw red and blue lights reflecting off the shrubbery and rock formations in the nearby landscaping. When he drew nearer he saw a fire truck and an ambulance at the front entrance. There also was a black van-type vehicle standing with its cargo doors open. Just as he approached the canopy at the building's front entrance the front doors slid open and a group of people, all dressed in blue coverall clothing came through. Some were carrying large bags and the others were pushing a gurney with someone all covered up on it. In the lobby, several housekeeping staff was standing together, and Craig inquired.

"Whom'd we lose today," he asked. A young lady whipping her eyes with a tissue responded.

"Miss Inge," she said. "Mr. Carson who lives below her heard a loud noise and called management. She had fallen. Looks like she got out of bed and tripped over her oxygen tubing. She had a big knot on her forehead. I always cleaned her room. Nice lady, I'm going to miss her."

When Craig reached the apartment, he could smell the fresh coffee before he opened the door. Martha was sitting at the kitchen table in her PJ's, a cup of coffee in hand watching the news on the local TV channel. There was a cup on the counter by the coffee pot.

"How was your walk this morning," Martha asked.

"It was a beautiful morning. The air was so clean and the sound of the river running and the smell of sage bushes beginning to turn green, it was nice." After pouring himself a cup of coffee he sat down across from Martha.

"We lost another resident this morning. It was someone you knew."

"None of my friends have been sick. Who was it?"

"It was that European lady, Inge Van Heusen."

"Oh No"! Martha exclaimed. "She and I were jewelry partners. She was on oxygen but when I saw her in the dining room yesterday she didn't appear to be ill. "What happened, do you know?"

"According to one of the staff, she might have hooked her leg in her oxygen tubing and tumbled."

"It's a little depressing," Martha said with a sigh. "Someone dies every week. Sometimes two or three. You get to know people in this place, they become more than just acquaintances, almost like family and then they're gone."

"You know this is a community," Craig stated. "Things happen here just like downtown or on a ranch, in the big city or any place else. We're just closer to things that happen."

"It's like this is God's waiting room," Martha mused.

"You feel that living in a place like this, we're just standing in line, waiting our turn?" Craig asked.

"The thought is a little depressing," Martha said.

"You know doll", Craig began. "Since we moved here we've met people that are here because their kids dumped them here. We've met people whose bodies have broken down as old horses do. Horses you would put down. Can't do that with Mom and Dad. They can't do it for themselves; the kids are so busy trying to make a life for themselves that they don't have time to babysit them. To make sure the old folks are safe and looked after, they put them in a place like this, some by mutual agreement, some because kids became parents, and they made the decision. Then there are those who looked ahead and realized that time is about to catch up to them and they give up living alone, keeping the property up, maybe making mortgage payments, cooking and washing dishes, moving a mile a minute, and going nowhere."

"I guess we fall into that last category," Martha said. "I certainly don't miss cooking and washing dishes and time is catching up." They both chuckled. "I'm really not complaining Craig. I'm glad we agreed to live here. I come and go as I please, if I please; I no longer have to worry about what you're into; we have people to visit with and we have lots of quality time just for ourselves."

"Yep", Craig agreed. "So when the time comes for us, we've had time to die."

"I don't know what that means but don't explain it," Martha said. "It's time for lunch, I'll get dressed and we'll get some food and see whom we can meet today."

As they entered the dining room for the noon meal, Martha noticed a lady sitting alone whom she had not seen before. She led the way to where the lady was sitting. As she neared the table she noticed that there were movements of the lady's body that seemed to be involuntary. Her neck would slide to the right or left, and she would bring it back to the center. Martha spoke to the lady.

"Would you mind if we joined you?"

"Not at all," was the reply. "I'd love to have you, pull up a chair."

"We are Martha and Craig Spence," Martha introduced themselves. "And your name is?"

"Cremair, Cremair Devin", was the reply. "My nickname is Kamer; You may call me that."

"That's a strange name," Craig observed. "I don't mean to be rude; I just never heard of a person with a name hung on them like that before. I grew up on a ranch and we had a horse we called Cream because he looked just like the cream that forms at the top of the milk bottles that the milkman delivered."

"When my mom was pregnant she had a craving for coffee creamers," Kamer said. "My dad said she drank them by the fist full. So when I was born my dad named me Cremair." My little sister couldn't say Creamair, so she called me Kamer, it stuck as my nickname. Please call me Kamer."

As Kamer talked, Craig noticed that her body from the waist up seemed to be slightly in constant motion. He recalled seeing that same sort of motion with a prisoner he once had who had Lou Gehrig's disease.

"You just move in?" Craig asked.

"Uh huh," Kamer said. "I came here from Alaska. After my husband died I had to find somewhere else to live. He was a commercial fisherman. I got this brochure in the mail one day and decided to try it. I sold the house to a newly married couple, the boat and stuff I sold to another fisherman and here I am." While Craig and Kamer were talking Martha was perusing the menu.

"There are two choices, fried chicken or spaghetti and meat sauce." She said to Craig.

"I guess I'll have the chicken," Craig said.

"And you?" Martha asked Kamer.

"Not crazy about either but I guess the Chicken," Kamer replied.

"I'll be the odd man out," Martha said. "I'm having the Spaget."

They were well into the meal when Martha could no longer contain her curiosity. So she whipped the red spaghetti sauce from her lips and addressed Kamer.

"I can't help but notice that you are never completely still. Is it something that you've had all your life?"

"No," Kamer responded. "It started several years ago. They don't know what it is. They've eliminated Lou Gehrig, but they think it might be some sort of Palsy. It has gradually gotten worse. I did contact a doctor in Denver, Colorado who reviewed my records and he is referring me to specialists in Minnesota. I'm waiting to hear from them. "

" So you have trouble getting around?" Martha asked. "I mean going shopping or just getting from place to place?"

"No", Kamer replied. "I still drive, and I use a walker when I'm out. My balance is terrible. Here in the Manor I seldom use my walker. I can hang on to the railings if I need to."

After they had finished eating and had had dessert, which was lemon meringue pie, Martha said to Kamer:

"Well, while you're getting settled in and getting to know your way around, our apartment number is 210, right across from the elevator. I'd love to hear about your life in Alaska and fishing for a living. "

"Thank you," Kamer responded. "I'd love to hear about being the wife of a sheriff for twenty years."

Since it was early spring and everything was coming to life, Craig decided to take a trip to the Wind River Mountain Range and photograph some scenery for his postcards. He and Martha agreed that he would take the trip on a day when she was working with jewelry and water coloring and such. According to AAA information, it would take him an hour and a half to get there, he could trace around for about three hours and get back home before dark.

The day before leaving, Craig went to the library and checked out a book titled "Wind River Range Wild Flowers. He anticipated that the hillsides and valleys would be covered, and he wanted to be able to identify them.

He left the Manor at sun up. As he neared the range the colors of the mountains were intoxicating. The sun's reflections of reds, yellows, and oranges on the rock formations across the top of the range and above the tree line were beautiful. There were still remnants of snow in the crevices along the ridge lines and it showed a baby pink in the sunlight.

Craig parked his jeep in a parking area at the base of Granite Peak trailhead and began a slow climb. The trail was not steep but had a gradual incline that suited Craig. Along the trail, he encountered a plant that grew on both sides and as he looked up ahead, the trail seemed to disappear in the plant growth and a mountain peak stood high above the tree tops making for a great picture. After capturing the scene he checked the book from the library, and it identified the plant as Elk Thistle.

Through an opening in the trees and foliage, he was able to look back at the trail he had traveled and the slope below it. There was a field of red, yellow, and pink flowers growing along the slope. He was able to identify the flowers as the Indian Paint Brush. They flower in different colors and are the Wyoming state flower according to the book.

The trail lead him out of the tree line onto a growth of Scrub Oak that served as a break between the trees and the rocky formations of the higher portions of the range. He hoped that the pictures would show the scene as he saw it. While he was taking in the view a deer emerged from the trees and stood looking directly at him. It was a doe. He didn't move and neither did she. After waiting a few minutes he took a picture, and the deer moved into the scrub. Craig still didn't move on because he knew that a lone doe would probably be on the lookout for more deer including a buck. Sure enough, three more doe and a buck with a magnificent rack stepped out into the scrub brush.

As he proceeded up the trail an odd feeling came over him. At one point the hair on the back of his neck stood up. Several times he stopped and surveyed the trees behind him and the rocks up ahead. There was a breeze now and it was getting colder. He decided it was best to start back down but as he turned to go he looked over the edge of the trail and saw a scene that was gorgeous. There was a valley, and it was covered with yellow, blue, and red flowers. A portion of his view of the valley was obscured by rocks and scrub bushes, He'd have to get up higher, he thought. Off the trail ways, he saw a rock formation that would serve as the perfect platform if he could climb to its top. It took a few minutes, but he managed to get to the flat top of the rock formation. It gave him a perfect view of the entire valley. He took a wide-angle lens from his camera bag and took several shots of the valley and the rocky peaks that stood beyond it.

After enjoying the view for a while, Craig decided to climb down and head back to Green River. As he got down on his hands and knees to put one leg over the edge of the rocks, he was facing an open space between several other rocks. The snow had melted just enough for him to recognize the horns and carcass of a deer. He took a few moments to look over the entire opening. There was what appeared to be half of a rib cage visible above the snow. He would have passed it off as part of the dead deer until he saw a half of a human skull sticking out of the snow a few feet away from the rib cage.

Craig repositioned himself, took out his camera, and took several pictures of what he could see. Through the camera lens, he could see what looked like pieces of cloth, perhaps pieces of a flannel shirt or scarf and pieces of a tattered brown material that could be pants or some outer garment.

He remembered the funny feeling he had back on the trail. The hair rose on his neck. He thought to himself, *was he being watched back there? Did I walk between some predator and his dinner, those deer that came out of the woods?* He carefully scoured the rocks and the surrounding area as he lowered himself from the rock formation. As he touched the ground he hurried to the trail which was in fairly open territory that allowed him to see a fairly good distance around himself.

He reached into the camera bag and took out his thirty-eight chiefs special that he always carried. He stared at it and thought, *If I get in trouble, this won't be much help.* He put it in his jacket pocket and started back down the trail. It seemed to take forever to get back to the Jeep. His heart had beat faster at every shadow, and cracking of branches caused by the wind that had come up or a bird that had fluttered close overhead.

Once back in Green River, Craig drove straight to the photo shop to have the film developed. He explained to the attendant that it was imperative that the film be developed immediately. He was allowed to wait while the film was processed.

Outside the store was a pay phone and Craig used the phone book hanging on a chain to call the Wind River Police Department. After explaining why he had called, it was arranged that someone from the Bureau of Indian Affairs would meet him back at the Manor sometime the following morning.

VII

Craig had finished his morning walk and was having coffee with Martha and discussing what he'd seen on his outing the previous day when there was a knock on the apartment door.

Martha, coffee cup in hand, In her bedroom slippers and robe, shuffled to the door.

"Who is it?" She inquired.

"Officer Malcolm Tanner, Ma'am. Bureau of Indian Affairs (BIA)," was the reply and Martha opened the door.

"Please, come in Officer Tanner. We've been expecting someone from your agency," Martha said. Craig left his chair and walked over and extended his hand to Officer Tanner.

"Hi ya, Hi ya Tanner," Craig said. "I'm Craig Spence and this is my wife Martha. Come, have a seat".

"Thank you sir", Tanner responded. "I don't expect that you remember me, but I was in the Academy graduating class that you addressed a few years ago,"

"No bull!" Craig exclaimed. "No, I don't remember anyone in a BIA uniform."

"No sir," Tanner responded. "I was with the Sublette County Sheriff's office at the time. I have an office up the road a piece in Pinedale, so I was detailed to this case."

"Would you like some coffee?" Martha asked.

"Would Love some, Ms. Spence," Malcolm answered, and Martha placed a steaming mug on the coffee table in front of him.

"I made my report to the Wind River Range Police Department," Craig advised. "How is it affiliated with the BIA?" He asked.

"The BIA runs the Wind River Range Police Department," Malcolm began. We can only arrest Native offenders. When a non-Native person breaks the law in the area we request assistance from the Wyoming Highway Patrol or the Sublette County Sheriff's Office. I was told that you came across human remains in the Range. Depending on where you found them will determine which protocol we proceed with in conducting an investigation. Most of the Wind Rivers is Tribal Land. Some of the land was sold to the State of Wyoming and the county or state Highway patrol has jurisdiction there. Do you have any idea where you were when you came across the remains?"

"I was on Granite Peak Trail, Craig started. I was probably two and a half miles up. I was taking pictures of the flowers that were growing on the sides of the foothills and in a valley. I had just passed the tree line and crossed a patch of scrub oak. I needed to get up high to get a wide swath of the valley, so I climbed a small rock formation and took some shots. When I turned to start down I spotted what I reported. Here are some pictures I took of the situation and there is a set that you can have."

Officer Tanner spread the photos over the coffee table and examined each one. After he had viewed each photo he spoke to Craig.

"Sir," he said. Do you by chance have a magnifying glass?"

"I have one," Martha said. "I use it to read prescriptions. It's getting harder and harder to read those things with the naked eye." She opened the drawer in a small desk in the corner of the room and brought out a square magnifying glass with a handle and handed it to Officer Tanner. He selected one of the photos and looked at it through the glass.

"In this picture, just off the trail, there are a couple of boulders," he said.

"Yeh." Craig agreed. "It was because of those boulders that I climbed that rock."

"Well," Tanner said as he moved the photo and the magnifying glass in front of Craig.

"Look right at the base of that boulder to the right in the photo," Tanner said. "You can just make out a cat that was watching you."

"Dang!" Craig exclaimed as he viewed the Photo. "Looks like I was being stalked."

"Climbing that rock just might have saved you a bad day," Tanner said. "Could you go with me to the area and show me where you were? I'll contact the Sheriff's Office and have them meet us at the trailhead."

"Sure, be glad too," Craig said. "Want to take a ride with me, Martha?"

"No, no," Martha said. "I'm going to see if I can find Mertel, haven't seen her in a while."

"Mertel's apartment was on the third floor, number 340. It was a little after four PM when Martha knocked on the door.

"Mertel, you home," she said.

"Who's that knocking at my door?" Came to the response from somewhere in the apartment.

"It's Martha, you home?"

"Just got in a few moments ago," Came a reply. "For you, I'm home." The door flew open and there was Mertel in her stocking feet and what appeared to be a cocktail in her hand. They gave each other a hug and Mertel led Martha to the kitchenette where she had kicked off her shoes. There was a small table with four chairs in the center of the room. On the table were a bottle of gin and a can of soda water.

"Didn't know you drank Mertel," Martha expressed surprise.

"Oh, I guess it's one of my little dirty secrets," Mertel said with a chuckle. "I sometimes have a pick me up when it's been a long day. Would you care for a toddy?"

"Thank you no," Martha declined. "If you have a pop I'll join you."

"Coke, Dr. Pepper, or Ginger ale," Mertel asked, and Martha chose the Ginger ale.

"Where have you been?" Martha asked as she popped the tab on the can.

"You know," Mertel began. "I've been meaning to call you; I've been leaving early and getting in rather late and just haven't gotten it done. I'm sorry, Forgive me?"

"What are you doing?" Martha asked. "Do you have a job or something?"

"No, well sort a," Mertel tried to explain. "I've been working with Milly."

"What! How come?" Martha asked.

"I spent a lot of time with her when she was in the hospital," Mertel started. "I took a liking to her and when she started her rehab she asked if I would work with her. Of course, I said yes. So I've been working with her every day. "

"How is she doing?" Martha asked, but she was thinking, *what is the rest of the story? Leaving early, getting home late, there's got to be more to this.*

"In the beginning it was tough," Mertel began. " She's a gutsy little lady. The exercises they gave her to do were very painful, but with my encouragement, she worked through the pain and tears and the anger at me for pushing her, and today there are no crutches. She's using a cane because her balance is a little shacky".

"Will she regain full use of that leg?" Martha asked.

"She'll have a little gimp in her get-go permanently. Lot of the muscle in that leg is gone and it'll always be a little weak." was Mertel's response. Placing the can of pop alongside her cheek, Martha tried to get a little more of the story from Mertel.

"You know Mertel, she said. "All day every day just doesn't compute for me. What else is going on?"

"I suppose you might say I'm the housekeeper for them". Mertel said. "I keep up the house, used to fix all of Milly's meals. She does for herself now. I help out where I can do shopping and laundry and stuff."

"Uh Hum," Martha mused. Then she said, "Gee, I think that is so nice of you, but you know, I've never thought of you as the housekeeper type. You gonna tell me what's going on or do I pour the rest of this pop down your blouse?"

" Martha," Mertel began. I haven't been this happy in a long time. Paul and I never had kids and I always longed to have a family. Those girls, we've become very close. They confide in me; they care about me, and I feel like I'm a part of the family I never had."

"There's another component to this family group that you've artfully avoided", Martha said. "Is there a relationship between Steve and you?"

"He's a sweetheart," Mertel said with a sigh. "He's getting used to me being around. I know he likes it when I'm around. I believe he feels more comfortable at work and is able to devote more quality time to his job because he knows I'm there."

"You didn't answer my question," Martha said, faking sternness.

"I'm working on it," Mertel said with a big grin on her face. Martha leaned across the table and took both of Mertel's hands in hers and said, "Go, Girl."

When Craig pulled into the parking lot at the trailhead, there were two all-terrain vehicles and a large white three-quarter-ton Dodge pickup already there. Both of the ATVs were marked with Sheriff's Department in big gold letters on the sides. The pickup had DIA stenciled on the doors. Officer Tanner got out of the Pickup.

"Good Morning Sir," he said. "These gentlemen are going to accompany us to the scene. This is Deputy Gordon Gomez and Deputy Terry Tanner, my nephew. If you will get in with Terry, I'll get with Gordon, and we'll head up."

Craig shook each deputy's hand and climbed into the passenger seat of the vehicle that Terry was driving. As they slowly headed up the trail he was amazed at how quiet the engine was. There was just a nice purring sound. Terry spoke first.

"Sir, I'm really honored to be the driver of a legend."

"What makes you think that son?" Craig quired.

"Everyone who goes through the academy nowadays gets a lecture about Sheriff Spence, the twenty-year sheriff of Sweetwater County, and his hard cover and soft covered books," Terry related.

"Never thought anybody outside of that class would remember," Craig said. "I talked to that class as a favor for a friend of mine. I wrote nothing down."

"Guess they forgot to tell you that everything is automatically recorded huh," Terry giggled.

"That's sneaky," Craig yelled. "It's Criminal." They both laughed aloud. It wasn't long before they reached the tree line and entered the scrub oak.

"Okay, slow down," Craig said. He pointed off to the right front and a short distance off the trail. "See that formation over there with the flat top? That's where I took some pictures. To the right of that formation is where the remains are." The vehicles were stopped at the rock formation and Craig led everyone on foot to the opening between the other rock formations. They stopped short of the remains. Deputy Gomez had a map and spread it on the ground, After he oriented it he spoke to announce his findings.

"We're on state land," he said. "The good news is, According to the map, the tribal lands start on a ridge a half mile further up. The bad news is the Sublette County line ends on the other side of Granite Peak Trail."

" Oh Boy," Tanner thought aloud. "The state boys are gonna love this." He took a hand radio from his belt and tuned it to the frequency of the Wyoming Highway Patrol. "We're pretty high here, I might be able to contact them and give them the bad news." Sure enough, he made contact and advised the dispatcher of the situation. After some minutes of back-and-forth conversation, he turned to the deputies. "They are getting together a forensic team and they figure they can be up here in couple-three hours. They want to know if you guys can stick around till then"?

"Wanna flip a coin to see who stays?" Terry suggested.

"No, no," Gomez said. "I'll stay down at the trailhead and wait for them. You go back and let the office know where I am and why. You'll just owe me one."

When Craig parked his jeep in his spot at the Manor, he noticed an ambulance at the front entrance. As he approached the front doors the medical crew was wheeling someone out on a gurney. The person was female, sitting up, but Craig didn't recognize her.

At the apartment he found Martha prone on the living room couch talking on the phone. When he closed the apartment door he heard her say to someone, "Well dear, Craig is home now and I'm anxious to hear about his trip. Take care and come see us."

"Hi ya Doll," he said as he tossed his hat on the coffee table and collapsed into one of the lazy boys.

"Long day, huh," Martha said as she picked up his cowboy hat and put it on her head. It was too big and flopped down around her ears. She posed and Craig laughed. "What happened out there."

"I took them to the place where I saw the remains. They determined that the location was on state property and called for the Highway Patrol to take over the investigation. They were sending a forensic team out when I left. What are we doing for supper?"

"We still have time to get served in the dining room, Wanna go?" Craig answered in the affirmative and they hurried to the elevator. The room appeared to be full. Craig always wondered at the bobbing heads and the multiple shades of gray. Periodically he would spot a full-headed blonde or a brunette and he enjoyed trying to determine if it were a wig or a treatment.

They spotted a table near the kitchen where the servers went in and out. They weaved their way to it. Once settled, Martha brought Craig up to date.

"You never mentioned anything, but did you notice that we never see Mertel around anymore?"

"Can't say I paid much attention," Craig responded.

"And had you noticed that the girls, Milly and Marla hadn't been around for some time?"

"I guess I have missed the girls, but I just figure they're busy being young people."

"Well, there's a connection," Martha paused while she let her comment sink in.

"You gonna tell me what the connection is, or do I have to guess?" Craig asked.

"Guess," Martha teased.

"Mertel and Steve have a thing," Craig said.

"What makes you say that?" Martha asked somewhat surprised.

"Well," Craig began. "When we were spending time with Milly at the hospital, Mertel was very attentive to Steve and his concerns. At that point he needed attention, and I thought she filled the bill."

"You're almost right," Martha said.

"What's up?" Craig asked.

"Mertel has been taking care of Milly through her recovery; working with her during her rehab every day; and she has become somewhat of the housekeeper. She and the girls have become very close. Though Steve enjoys having her around he's not made any overtures. She's got her sights on him. I had a long visit with her today and I was on the phone with Milly when you came in a while ago." She looked over at Craig and he had an impish smile on his face.

"How is she doing?" Craig asked.

"Pretty well she says," Martha responded. " She's put up her crutches and is using a cane now. In another week she's planning to return to work part-time."

"These young'uns mend fast don't they?" Craig shook his head in amazement.

It was on a Saturday while Craig was watching the University of Wyoming Track and Field event on TV that he got a call from Officer Tanner. They exchanged greetings and small talk before Tanner explained the reason for his call.

"Sheriff Spence, (most law enforcement people occasionally still called Craig Sheriff). I thought you'd like to be brought up to date on your find in the Wind Rivers," Tanner began. "That forensic team found other bones scattered around the area and determined that the remains belonged to a human female, approximately forty to fifty years old, and estimated that they had been there for some time. So whatever happened probably took place over a year ago."

" There were no missing person reports during that period?" Craig asked.

" Apparently none that the Coroner was aware of," Tanner replied. "We'll have to dig a little more to determine if there was and to what agency."

"Did they find anything else?" Craig asked. "What about clothing and such?"

"There was very little left of the clothing that could help in identifying the remains," Tanner advised. "They conducted a hundred-yard search around the sight, and they located the remnants of what appeared to be a small backpack. In the vicinity of the pack, there were several tools. They found a small pick-like tool, a small scope, and a chisel. The Pack had been ripped up pretty well but this is the interesting part. There had been a plastic card holder on it and a piece of the card was still stuck to the plastic. They were able to discern the name of Peggy. The rest of the card was erased by weather or ripped away."

"Hold on Malcom," Craig said with some excitement. Under the Coffee table was the book he had checked out of the library to identify the flowers. He opened it to the last pages on which there was the authors biography. The name of the author was Peggy Mortenson.

"Malcom, I checked out a library book to be able to tell the names of the flowers I was taking pictures of. The name of the author was Peggy Mortenson."

"What else does it say about her Sheriff?" Officer Tanner wanted to know.

"I'll just read it to you", Craig said.   *Peggy Mortenson was born Peggy Jenson, on August 25*[th]*, 1947, in the small mining town of Ouray, Colorado. She graduated from a school of higher learning in South Dakota with a degree in Geology. In 1975 she married Cory Mortenson, the owner of a small ranch near the Wind River Mountains in Wyoming. After Mr. Mortensons death in 1980, Peggy moved to Silver Cliff Colorado where she explored old mining digs long abandoned. Every summer Peggy returned to the ranch and spent the month of June studying the rock formations and authoring books about the Wind River Range and articles for geological magazines.* " What do you know about that ranch Malcom?"

" I've heard about the old Mortenson Ranch," Malcom said. "I've never been out there myself. I'll pass the information on to the Patrol boys. Thanks Sheriff, I'll talk with you later."

VIII

An invitation extended by Martha brought Steve Lolly and his daughters Milly and Marla to the Manor for dinner. It was a weekend and Steve didn't have to be too concerned about what was going on at the Detention Center. Marla processed passengers on the weekend flight in the morning and there were no weekend classes at the community college so she could have a relaxing evening also. Milly had her daily exercise routine that she dutifully engaged in during the afternoon so she could relax and hang out too. Craig and Martha met them in the lobby of the Manor.

"Hi Ya, Hi ya, you guys," Craig greeted them and put his arm around Steve's shoulder. Martha gave each of the girls a big hug and then led the group into the dining room. Once seated Martha was interested in what was going on in the girls lives.

"Don't see much of you two anymore," She said to the girls. "Are things going well for you?" Marla spoke up.

"I really apologize," She began. "I doubled up on my credits at community because I've been accepted at UW at Laramie, and I start this fall. I'll have the majority of the pre-requisites behind me. It's been a tough slog, but it'll pay off I think. Thanks to Mertel taking over most of the house work and stuff so I could really devote all my time to studies."

"Mertel was telling me that she was spending considerable time with you all," Martha related. "She also told me that she cracked the whip keeping you on course with your rehab Milly. How's that coming?"

"I have nothing but respect for that lady," Milly responded. "There were times when I was ready to just quit, didn't want to deal with the pain or put in the effort, and she was there for me, egging me on, encouraging and sometimes chastising. She kept me going and I've come a long way. I may have to use this cane for a while, but I can walk. I have Mertel to thank for it."

"She's been an angel sent from heaven", Steve interjected. She just took over and we're all better for it."

"Sounds like you've all taken a liking to each other," Craig observed.

"Steve," Martha inquired. "Has it become more than just someone who manages the household?" The question caught Steve off guard, and he hesitated to respond. He thought a moment before he did.

"You know Martha," he began. "After Kathy passed away, I never thought there would be any one to take care of things and look after us, no one to fill that void in our lives. Mertel has just grown on us. We're blessed that she has come to us."

"I asked Mertel the same question," Martha pursued. "She too artfully danced around and avoided a direct answer. All these years Steve you've been like a son to us, and I want to know. Is there or could there be a relationship building between you and Mertel?" Marla and Milly joined in.

"Yeh Dad," Marla said. "What about it?"

"Great question Martha," Milly said. "Come on Dad, cough it up. We want to know too." Steve looked at Craig who was sitting quietly across the table from him, with that -don't look at me- expression on his face.

"I've never really thought about it," Steve confessed. "I like her a lot, like having her around, but I have no idea how she feels." Craig finally spoke up.

"You damn sure won't know if you don't ask her, Steve. Look standing in the door way."

Everyone turned to look at the dining room entrance and there was Mertel, surveying the room for a place to sit. Marla stood and beckoned her to come sit with them. Craig found an empty chair at another table and made room for it.

"Well, must be my lucky day," Mertel said. "All of my favorite people in one place at the same time. Thanks for making room for me." The girls and she exchanged hugs and Martha, and she clasped hands. Before taking her seat she rubbed the top of Craigs head and sat in the chair Steve was holding for her.

While everyone was getting settled the server was standing by to take their dinner order. They had a choice between Salisbury Steak, Mashed Potatoes and Green Beans or Barbequed Ribs with the same veggies. Everyone chose the Barbequed Ribs.

Everyone enjoyed finger eating their ribs, chatting in between bites, and licking their fingers. Steve and Craig caught up on things in the world of law enforcement and Steve advised Craig that Sherrie, the jail administrator, had retired. The ladies acquainted each other with new stores now in the Mall and where they could save the most money on purchases that they could make. After dessert, which was Coca Cola cake, Martha suggested that Craig tell everyone about his latest adventure.

"Craig has been collecting pictures of spring life for his post cards," she said. "flowers and animals with their young and such. He took a trip to the Wind Rivers. You take it from there Craig."

"It was a great day to be outside," Craig began. "I took a trail up through the range, taking pictures of the flowers and colors, rock formations and a small deer heard that popped out of the trees. From where I was standing I could see across a valley and you can't believe the scene; flowers of all colors, blues, reds, yellows and purples all through the valley and up the foot hills on the other side. To get the best shot I needed to get higher, so I climbed a rock formation that was several yards off the trail and got some great shots. When I started down, I saw an open space between some other rocks and there was the carcass of a deer. I could see the horns sticking up out of snow that hadn't melted completely yet. A little further into the opening I saw what appeared to be part of a rib cage. Looking through a telephoto lens I could see clearly that it was a rib cage and there was a skull nearby that was undoubtedly human," Craig said.

"I took pictures of the remains and came back to town. I had the film processed and called the Wind River PD. The next morning an officer from the Bureau of Indian Affairs came to see me and looked at my pictures. He spotted something that I hadn't noticed." He paused and looked over at Martha.

"There were some tall rocks that forced me to get higher in order to capture the entire scene. Using Martha's magnifying glass, the officer saw between two boulders, a Mountain Lion- in stealth posture- looking in my direction. Either it was stalking me, or it was stalking those deer that came out of the trees, and I just happened to walk between them and it- I don't know- but things could have gotten exciting."

"Wow"! Steve exclaimed. " Even in retirement you still generate excitement, boss."

"I've decided that I need to upgrade my fire power if I'm going to be out in the wild," Craig said. My Chief Special ain't gonna cut it."

"I've got a 357 Mag at home," Steve said. "I don't use it anymore and it's just the ticket for your needs. You can have it. I'll bring it by sometime."

"I need an excuse to stop in and visit folks down and around the Center, just take it to your office and I'll stop by and pick it up while I'm visiting," Craig said.

Steve then turned to Mertel. "Before you came in, the conversation was how great it was that you were being such a help to the girls and me. Marla and Milly really appreciate all you do for us. Everyone here feels that you and I should be an item."

"So do I," Mertel responded. Everyone at the table began to applaud. "What do you think Steve? That's what's important."

"I've actually wanted to approach the matter with you for some time," Steve confessed. "Kept putting it off. I'm a little out of practice about these things. I also was really concerned about what the girls would think. Guess I don't have to worry about that any more. What say we head up to Jackson Hole next week end and feel each other out?"

"Out of Practice huh?" Mertel commented. "Sounds like a come on to me and I've been out of the market for years. I don't have any plans for next weekend and if I did I'd cancel them. You're on. "

Along with an officer from the Wyoming Highway Patrol, Malcom Tanner drove out to the Mortenson Ranch. The Ranch sat in a picturesque setting in a valley, bordered on two sides by sand stone rock formations. According to records at the Sublette County Assessor's Office, the ranch consisted of two hundred acres of agricultural land. There was a stream that meandered right down the middle of the property.

The road to the ranch was in reasonably good condition and there were vehicle tracks. Someone obviously either lived at the ranch or possibly trespassers had frequented the place. The patrolman, George Stephens, suggested that Malcom proceed at a very slow speed so as not to rush in and be surprised. A slow approach gave them time to get a good visual of conditions and any activity that might develop. People living out in these outlying areas don't take kindly to uninvited visitors George advised Malcom.

As they rounded a curve in the road they saw up ahead a clump of Douglas Fir trees. The Douglas Firs protected a two-story house that had a porch across the front. There was an older model pickup in what could be considered the front yard. On the porch stood a man and a woman. The man, dressed in jeans, to include a jean jacket, stood wide legged, rifle in hand while the woman in buckskin attire, stood holding a leash that was attached to a beautiful full grown Doberman Pincher.

When Malcom brought the truck to a stop, George stuck his arm out of the passenger side window and waved to the couple. There was no response. They chose to exit the truck slowly and George, who was in full uniform, was the first to speak.

"Good day to you," He said. "I'm officer Stephens from the Wyoming Highway Patrol, and this is officer Tanner from the Bureau of Indian Affairs, and we're here to see Peggy Mortenson." The woman turned and let the dog into the house and the man with the rifle laid the rifle against the wall and came out to the truck.

"I'm Wox," he said. "My Wife, Little Owl. Come sit with me." He led the way to some benches at the corner of the house. Little Owl came to join them. Wox continued. "We have been care takers for this ranch for many years. We worked for Mortenson. When he die, Peggy moved away and told us to stay."

"Peggy come back every year," Little Owl began. "She write or take the horse and go to the mountain and get rocks. Two years ago, she come, she took the horse and go longer than most times. The horse come back. Not Peggy."

"Did you look for her?" Malcom asked.

"The horse have all of Peggy's gear on him. Her 30-30 rifle was in the scabbard; the saddle bags with food and bottles of water; extra shirt and light jacket; her bed roll, everything was still there. I took the horse and looked till darkness. I come back and tell Sheriff's people. They looked for her, then a storm came, winds blew, and snow fell. It got very cold. They stopped looking. I often go back but I don't find Peggy."

"What do you think happened to her," George asked.

"I think, maybe, something spooked the horse. she fall off and was hurt. The horse run away," Wox said. Malcom turned to George.

"From where we found the remains, if it turns out to be Peggy, she could have crawled back there between those rocks for protection from the storm."

"Yeh," George agreed. "There was still some hair attached to that skull we found." George turned to Wox. "Is there a hair brush or a comb that Peggy used still around."

"We leave everything just as it was," Little Owl said. "Come with me, I show you."

Little Owl led the officers through a large living space with rough western style furniture. The dog lay on a rug in front of a fire place. A room most likely used as an office had a long table still littered with papers, books, and rocks. There was a manuscript still there as Peggy had left it, unfinished. A small book-like item was also on the table. This turned out to be a diary in which Peggy recorded her daily activities and her thinking.

In a small bedroom, there was a small bed, a dresser with books stacked on it, a ceramic wash bowl and a large ceramic pitcher. Everything in the bed room was clean. Little Owl kept it clean. "A place for her spirit to sleep," Little Owl said. On a small table next to the bed was a hair brush, some elastic ties, like women use to tie their hair in a pony tail, a Bible and a small butane lamp. George picked up the hair brush and the diary, put them into sandwich bags that he got from little Owl and decided to leave everything else as was.

Malcom decided to have the records checked at the Sublette County Sheriff's office to see if he could better pin down when the disappearance of Peggy Mortenson happened. There was a missing person's report. It was determined that on June 16, 1986, a missing person's report was filed by the caretakers at the Mortenson Ranch…

According to the report, Peggy Mortenson had traveled by horse back into the Wind River Range. When the horse returned without her, the caretaker took the horse and tried to retrace its tracks. Tracking was difficult, many horses passed through that day and there was nothing peculiar about the hooves of Peggy's horse. The caretaker searched till dark and then filed a missing person's report at eleven-forty PM on June 16, 1986.

The Sublette County Sheriffs Pose, a volunteer unit made up of former deputies and local county residents ventured into the Mountains at sun rise June 17, 1986. Without any specific information as to where Peggy Mortenson might have gone, the volunteers fanned out on horseback, two persons to a party and covered as much territory as possible before sun set. During the night, a summer storm formed, dropping temperatures and blowing snow blanketed the area with six to ten inches. The search was called off until conditions improved. Follow up reports indicated that volunteers, hoping to make a recovery, had made several sorties thereafter with no success...

In most multi living complexes the center for social activity and community togetherness is a club house, a community center or a community hall. So it was at the Senior Manor of Green River. Although there was an activity space where games were played, Bible studies and discussion sessions were held; adult coloring, painting, jewelry and greeting card designing and such took place; a chapel and small movie theatre; the place most enjoyed by residents was the dining room.

Meal time in the Manor dining room was like a social hour. Residents visited and hugged one another as if they hadn't seen each other for some time. They laughed at and with one another, joshed and complemented on each other's hair do, nails, choice of jewelry and attire. There was much to do about health conditions and medical appointments and procedures. No one sat around as if they were just waiting to die.

Craig and Martha was among those who enjoyed mealtimes at the Manor. Meeting new people and touching base with previous acquaintances was looked forward to by Martha. Craig was a people watcher and enjoyed observing how people conducted themselves, their eating habits, listening to the unpleasant complaints about food choices being served and admiring people with physical disabilities keeping on in spite of their difficulties. So it was this day at the evening meal.

Craig and Martha had already seated themselves when a petit lady with a walker and on oxygen approached the table.

"Hi", she said. "you two want some company"? She had a small mouth and a very engaging smile.

"If the company is a pretty lady with a walker and a cute smile, we'd love it," Craig responded. "I'm Craig and my wife Martha," he said as he took Martha's hand in his. "What's the name of our company?"

"I'm Clara, Clara Mills," the little lady said as she parked her walker beside the table and adjusted the plastic tubing from the Oxygen Concentrator so that there was less pressure on her ears. She took a seat next to Craig and directly across the table from Martha.

Clara was probably five foot, more or less. Like most people at the Manor she had greying hair. It hung straight down around her head and was cut even with her jaw line. She wore a pair of granny style glasses and tiny angel ear rings. She was dressed in a jean outfit that really looked good on her, Martha thought. Clara also had a slight curvature in her upper back.

"Well Clara, how long have you been here?" Martha inquired. "I don't recall seeing you around. Love your earrings by the way."

"Thanks. Haven't been here before," Clara said with a giggle. "I'll be moving in tomorrow. My daughter is a nurse at the hospital, so I've been staying with her. The truck with my furniture arrives tomorrow."

"Where are you coming from?" Craig asked.

"Just down the road in Evanston," Clara replied. "I lost my husband last month and decided to be near my daughter. Thought I'd come over and check out the food."

"Sorry to hear that," Martha was sympathetic. "Must be hard."

"No," Clara began. "He was in hospice for over a year. He didn't recognize any of us anymore. He had forgotten how to do things; didn't know when to go to the bathroom; slowly he stopped talking; stopped eating and finally stopped being able to breath. He's at a much better place."

"How long were the two of you together?" Craig asked.

"Sixty-Five years," Clara said. "That's not including the year he was in hospice."

"How long have you been on oxygen?" Craig was curious.

"A little over six months," Clara replied. "Came down with a lung infection that caused some damage and now I have to carry my friend, the concentrator, everywhere I go."

"Doesn't seem to slow you down any," Martha said.

"It's a little inconvenient, but it is what it is," Carla replied.

IX

ne of Craig's treasured activities in retirement was his early morning walks on days when the weather wasn't nasty. The air was cool and crisp; the sun rising - painting the cirrus clouds in the sky with yellows, reds and shades of pink. This morning he was especially rewarded because he had come across two ground owls standing outside their burrow. He spent a few moments watching them watch him. They brought back memories of being out on the ranch as a boy. There were lots of these little critters with their sandy coloring, long legs and bright yellow eyes.

His other encounter on this particular morning was a family of deer. A doe, a buck and a fawn were taking in water on the opposite side of the river. As he continued slowly along the path, the doe stood at alert, her attention focused on him while the fawn made short jumping bursts around the two adults. The buck lowering his head to take quick sips of water and raising just high enough to get a look at Craig across the river. In the early morning sunlight they looked like images on a greeting card.

On his way back to the apartment he picked up a copy of the local newspaper from a stand at the front desk. The headlines caught his attention.

"RETIRED SHERIFF LOCATES REMAINS OF MISSING GEOLOGIST"

At the top of the column was a file picture of him in his ever-worn cowboy hat with a badge front and center. Right under the picture was printed in small letters- *sheriff Craig Spence (retired)*. He folded the paper and hurried to the elevator. As he entered the apartment he called out to Martha:

"Hey Doll, where are ya?"

"In the kitchen," Martha called back.

"Look at the headline in today's paper," he said as he laid the paper on the table in front of her.

" Were you aware that a positive ID had been made?" Martha asked.

" No, I haven't heard from Malcom for a couple of weeks," Craig said. They both began to read the article.

"The Bureau of Indian Affairs in conjunction With the Sublette County Sheriff's office have confirmed that remains found in the Wind River Mountain Range are those of Peggy Mortenson, a Geologist and part time resident of the Mortenson Ranch located between the Shoshone Reservation and State-owned land in the Wind River Range. In 1986 a missing person's report was filed when Ms. Mortensons horse returned from the mountains without her. Searches by Sublette County failed to locate Ms. Mortenson. According to a news release from the Department of Indian Affairs, human remains were located by Sheriff Craig Spence (retired) who was on a photo excursion to the Range. A state forensic team has positively identified the remains as being those of Peggy Mortenson."

The article continued on, detailing how the positive identification was made using the hair fossils found at the scene and from a hair brush used by Ms. Mortenson. Confirmation of their finding was made through dental records obtained from a dentist in the town where she lived in Colorado. According to the investigators report, Information in a diary kept by Ms. Mortenson led investigators to a next of kin. A son, Clark Mortenson who is an Anthropologist at a University in Europe.

As Craig pulled into the parking lot of the County Detention Center, he spotted an old familiar sign in one of the parking spaces. It read: **SHERIFF – DON'T EVEN THINK ABOUT PARKING HERE-** That sign had been posted to reserve his parking space for twenty years and it still brought a smile to his face when he'd see it. He found an empty space, parked and entered the building through the main entrance. There was only a few people in the foyer. Probably waiting to see an inmate. At the front desk , there was Heather, the receptionist. She was busy at her computer when Craig walked up and spoke.

"Can a person get a little service around here," he said and as Heather swung around in her chair to face him he noticed that she was really pregnant.

"Sheriff Spence"! She exclaimed as she waddled around the desk to give him a hug. "My goodness it's good to see you. It's been a while."

"So I see," Craig said. "you're more gorgeous than ever. When's the little guy due?"

"Actually. I'm overdue," Heather said with a grimace and a turned-up lip. "How'd you know it's a boy?"

"Girls don't need that much room," Craig said with a chuckle. "Is the old crew around?"

"Sheriff Lolly is in his office and Kevin should be around," Heather advised.

"What about Sherrie?" Craig asked.

"Oh, you probably hadn't heard," Heather said. "She retired a few months ago. She moved to Nebraska where her sons are."

"Now that you mention it, I remember Steve mentioning it," Craig remembered. "Who's in charge?"

"Deputy Maggie Harris,' Heather responded. "you might remember she was one of the deputies that found that Brown had killed Watson in their cell a few years back."

"What a deal that was," Craig said. "Then Brown escapes and we chased him all over the county. I'll never forget that. He almost did me in too. Yeh, I remember Maggie. If you'll buzz me in I'll go harass your boss."

Steve was on the phone when Craig stood in front of the open door to his office. Craig patiently waited until Steve hung up the phone.

"Hey Boss," Steve said in greeting. "Come on in and sit."

"Thought I'd come by and check you out Steve, "Craig said. "How goes it?"

"I was just on the phone with the comptroller out in Indiana, Steve replied. "It's been a long-drawn-out process getting reimbursed for shipping Normans body back there. Think we've got it squared now."

"Not only does justice move slowly, so does payment for services, Huh?" Craig commented.

"Yep," Steve agreed. "By the way, I've got that revolver we were talking about." Reaching in the lower draw of his desk, Steve removed a holstered 357 Magnum and handed it to Craig. He then walked over to a filing cabinet and took a box of 357 cartridges and placed it on the desk in front of Craig. "This should fix you right up."

"Thanks Steve. Have you heard from Sherrie since she left?" Craig asked.

"Yes Sir," Steve responded. "She's called in a couple of times. She being a grandma to one of her sons kids back in Nebraska. He is a general Contractor back there. Her other son is back there too, he's got a landscaping company and he has no kids."

"Wow!" Craig exclaimed. I never thought those two would ever amount to much. She had a hard time raising them by herself. Guess you never know."

"You had a lot to do with them kids, boss," Steve commented. "When you hired her on you spent a lot of time keeping them boys on the straight and narrow. I guess something you gave them must have stuck."

After taking a tour of the facility with Steve and shaking hands with staff still on the job, Craig decided that he should go and visit the County Attorney's Office. Some of his most memorable projects had been through his affiliations with Sarah Cousins, the County Attorney.

When he entered the old county building a flood of memories from the many years he walked those floors flowed back. As he passed offices he glanced through the large glass windows with sandblasted names, *Sweetwater County Assessor's Office, Sweetwater County Clerk's Office, Sweetwater County Road & Bridge, Sweetwater County District Attorney's Office, Sweetwater District Court,* and finally *Sweetwater County Attorney's Office.*

Nancy, the receptionist, saw Craig through the plate glass window and met him on the run as he came through the door. She wrapped her arms around his neck and gave him a bear hug, knocking his hat off his head.

"My hero," she said. "I hadn't seen you for so long I thought you were gone forever."

"Hi ya Doll?" Craig said regaining his balance. "If I'd known you'd miss me this much I'd come by sooner."

"Sarah, look who's here." Nancy called out.

"What for heaven's sake is all the commotion out here," Sarah said as she came from her office. Seeing Craig, she threw open her arms and hurried to embrace him. "You don't know how good it is to see you after all this time." *Sarah had not aged well,* Craig thought. Her face was drawn, she had lost weight and as she hugged him he thought he felt a slight tremor. Now, as she drew back a bit he could look into her eyes. That look of confidence and control he remembered wasn't there.

"Hi ya, Doll?" Craig said." How's the best darn County Attorney in Sweetwater County?"

"In case you've forgotten, I'm the only County Attorney in Sweetwater County," she said with a halfhearted smile. "Come, hope you have a minute to visit." Sarah led Craig into her office and seated him at a small meeting table. She drew up a chair and gingerly sat herself.

"Tell me?" she asked. "How's retirement? Do you wish you'd have stayed a little longer?"

"Until I left office," Craig said as he took off his hat and placed it on the table. "I had no idea how much stress was involved in the job I loved. I haven't missed the politics and the frustrations of dealing with politicians. The people, my staff and professionals like yourself, yeh- I missed that comradery and the accomplishments we achieved together. I have never had the desire to come back though. I've been able to spend quality time with Martha, see other than the worst in people, travel a little and enjoy doing stuff I've never had time to do before. To answer your question, retirement for me is good, but tell me about you. How goes it for you?"

"As you well know, being the County Attorney has been a blast. I've learned so much in the time I've been here, but time hasn't been kind to me. Not too long after you left office I began to feel different physically. My balance became iffy, I seemed to slow down, didn't move as usual. Then I noticed my hand writing was really getting bad, there was just a slight trembling in my hands." She laid her hands flat on the table and Craig could see that her fingers would not stay flat. There was slight movement, independently the fingers on her hands would twitch slightly. She continued. "I finally went to see my doctor and after a battery of tests I was diagnosed with Parkinson's."

"That's a tough hand to be dealt, Sarah," Craig said sympathetically.

" That's what I thought too," Sarah said. "For a few months I was an emotional mess, but then the doctors told me that it would be a slow progression and it might take years for it to get to the point that I may not be able to function, or it might not get that bad. I'm so glad that you came by today because you've made me realize that I've made the right decision. I've given the county notice that I'm resigning. By God I'm gonna whoop it up as long as I can and follow you. I've got a bucket list. There are some places I want to see, some things I want to do and I'm going to do them while I can."

"That sounds like the Sarah I remember," Craig said. "I'm really sorry to hear that this has happened to you Doll. You know my dad used to say, "*When you walk through the bushes, you'll probably get full of cockle burrs. You just stop for a minute, pick em off and go on.*" That's the way getten through life is. Nobody said living would be without them cockle burrs but we gotta go on. Good Luck to ya Doll. Give it hell."

After his visit with Sarah, his trip back home was somber. What was happening to her really tugged at his heart strings. She was in the prime of life and it was slowly being squeezed out of her. *Why does such bad things happen to such good people,* he asked himself.

When he got home to the apartment at the Manor, Martha met him with some good news. Katie was coming home for the weekend. She had called and said that the person she was the care taker for had passed away a few days ago and she would have some time off while the company she works for finds another client for her. She left Thermopolis this morning, will visit with a friend in Lander tonight and come the rest of the way tomorrow…

Lander, Wyoming was a little over a hundred miles to Green River, Wyoming. That equates to a little over a two-hour drive should weather not be a problem. Katie left the day before calling her mother, before sunup, hoping to be well on her way before the eighteen wheelers that travel that route got under way.

She had bought herself a used nineteen eighty-three Volkswagen Bug that was a scrambled egg yellow a few months before taking this trip and she was anxious to see what it would be like on the open road. She would have a short climb of the south eastern corner of the Wind River Mountain Range, but the rest would be level or downhill.

After an hour and a half on the road, Katie felt that she needed to find a place that had rest room facilities. Low and behold a road sign proclaimed, **"BITTER CREEK REST AREA 3 MILES"** and she could see it up ahead. After what seemed like an awful long time she parked in the area for automobiles and entered the building. As she rounded the passage way to the ladies rest room she thought she heard a baby crying. Making her way to a stall she listened, and she heard it again. It's not a baby she thought, there were two distinct whimpering sounds coming from one of the stalls. While washing her hands at one of the sinks installed along the wall she heard someone speak.

"We're so stupid. We should never have done this," and the whimpering began again. Katie decided to see what was going on. She began to tap on the door of the stall that the sounds were coming from.

"Hello in there," she said. "Are you okay?" The whimpering stopped but there was no response. "Come on, open the door. If you need help maybe I can help you." After waiting a minute she heard the bolt slide and the door slowly opened. Two young girls crouched together; each sharing half of the toilet seat stared out at her. One, with straight blond hair that hung strait down to her shoulders and brown eyes appeared to be the older of the two. The other, a brown curly top with freckles and pale blue eyes had her hands up covering her face and crying. Both were dressed in long dresses. They had a well-worn blanket wrapped around their shoulders.

"What's going on?" Katie asked and the older one spoke up.

"We're lost and we're hungry and we have no place to go."

"How did you get here?" Katie asked.

"Freight Train," came the response.

"What"! Katie exclaimed. "Where?" she asked. The girl with the straight blond hair pointed in a southerly direction.

"There are train tracks over there. The train slowed down and we jumped off," she said.

"Out here in the middle of nowhere, Why did you jump off?" Katie asked. "Why were you on that train in the first place?"

"CeCe's brother, this is Celine, we call her CeCe. Her brother Daniel said he was going to run away from home. We said we'd go too. So we all got on the train together."

"Come out of there," Katie said sternly. "You guys are filthy. Let's see if we can clean you up a bit." Using paper towels from the dispensers Katie scrubbed the grim off their faces and had each to wash their hands. Their dresses were a mess too but that would have to wait.

"See that yellow car over there?" Katie said as she pointed to her VW. "Come get in, you're coming with me. By the way, if she's CeCe, what's your name?"

" Beth, the older girl said. "Please don't call our parents, it will be bad for us."

"We'll talk about that later," Katie said as she arranged them in the back seat of the VW. The younger of the two had started sniffling again. "Don't cry dear, for now the worst is over." Once established back on the road Katie again questioned the girls.

"How old are you Beth?" She asked.

"Fourteen," was the response.

"And you CeCe? How old are you?" Katie wanted to know.

"I'm twelve," the curly top said.

"Why did the two of you get off the train?" Katie asked.

"We were cold last night, and we were hungry," Beth said. "We started crying and told Daniel that we wanted to go back. He said that if we didn't shut up and stop crying he was going to beat us. So when we got the chance we jumped."

"How old is Daniel and where is he?" Katie asked.

"He's Sixteen," CeCe responded. "I don't know where he is. He stayed on the train. Where are you taking us?"

"I'm on my way to see my parents. I'm not leaving you out here. I'm taking you with." Katie said matter of factly. "Where did you get on the train Beth?"

"Sweetwater, Texas," Beth responded.

"That's kind of funny," Katie replied. "You got on in Sweetwater, Texas and jumped off in Sweetwater County, Wyoming." That brought a giggle from the girls.

"When and why did you decide to run away?" Katie asked.

"We didn't decide, Daniel did," CeCe said.

"But you decided to go along, Why?" Katie pursued her questioning. Beth tried to explain.

"Our families belong to the same church group. That's how we know each other, and we go to the church school together. Our parents are really strict. My dad drinks a lot. He always wants me to pour him his beer. If I pour and it runs over the top of the glass he slaps me. If I do the dishes after supper and I break a dish he beats me. If I don't clean up like he likes, he beats me. If I talk to a boy, when I get home he beats me."

"What about your mother, Beth?" Katie asked.

"She tries to protect me sometimes," Beth said , coming to tears. "But then she gets beat too."

"My Mom beats Daniel," CeCe said. "She beats him with a crop like what horse riders use. Sometimes, I don't know why she beats him, she just does."

"Does she beat you too CeCe?" Katie asked as she watched her through the rear-view mirror.

"Nope, just Daniel," CeCe said.

"You hang out with your brother a lot CeCe?" Katie asked.

"Next to Beth he's my best friend," CeCe responded…

As she drove into Green River, Katie stopped at a convenience store where there was a pay phone. She called her parents' number. Martha answered the phone.

"Hello," she said.

"Mom, this is Katie. I think I've done something dumb," Katie confessed. She went on to tell Martha the story about finding the run aways and deciding to bring them with her. "The closer I got to Green River the less I thought of the idea," Katie revealed.

"Hang on a minute Katie," Martha said. She covered the mouth piece with her hand and turned to Craig who was watching the evening news on TV. "Prepare yourself," she said. "Katie's bringing home two runaways that she picked up at a rest stop." Martha then returned to the phone conversation. "Katie," she said. "Over the years you've done a few things of which I didn't approve. If you hadn't done this I'd be ashamed of you. Where are you anyway?"

"I'm at a pay phone Mom, I'll be there in a few minutes," Katie advised.

When Martha hung up the phone she heard the microwave beep. Craig was unwrapping another pack of frozen hamburger meat.

"I'll cook the hamburgers if you'll take care of the fixens," he said, and Martha began bringing lettuce, and tomatoes from the fridge to the kitchen counter. She paused a minute and looked at Craig. She smiled approvingly . *What a guy*, she thought.

THE END